TAYLOR AND THE FINAL NINE

THE ITURIA CHRONICLES

J.B. MOONSTAR

TAYLOR AND THE FINAL NINE

THE ITURIA CHRONICLES

J.B. MOONSTAR

DEDICATION

My thanks to Peter and Indy for their support of Ituria's Alliance!

Dear Reader,

One of Ituria's main goals is to rescue endangered animals, saving them from death at the hands of man. In my continuing chronicles of interactions between Ituria's realm and the human world, I relate the continuing adventures of a young boy and his courage to protect those in need, even if the likelihood of success seems impossible.

After assisting in the rescue of a red wolf family, Taylor was given a magic feather that allows him to communicate with the animals he meets in the wilderness. He uses this magical feather to help animals understand how to keep safe from humans, and to rescue them when they call for help.

One area he patrolled as often as possible was a local riverside beach, noting that hermit crabs and other local animals get trapped by discarded plastic and glass, so he makes sure to rescue every creature he finds. While on his rounds, he discovers that poachers have trapped one of the few remaining red wolves and he is unable to set it free.

How can he get help before the poachers get back? Who can he ask to help him? Only time will tell if he has enough courage and spirit to succeed in his quest. Follow Taylor's adventures where one step leads to another, until standing up to the poachers is his only option.

Sincerely,

Knocker,

First Guard to Ituria

Table of Contents

Chapter One

HERMIT CRAB RESCUE

"Hi guys, I'm back!" Taylor called out as he walked onto a short stretch of sandy beach hidden by a large row of trees. Using his bike for balance, he walked along the riverbank, a mixture of sand, small pebbles, and some larger stones. Almost every day he visited here, patrolling a little portion of the beach at a time, as he noticed trash would constantly wash up on the beach—empty bottles, cans, plastic bags—all sorts of traps for unsuspecting little creatures.

Stopping next to a large glass bottle half submerged in the sand near the water's edge, he put the kickstand down so the bike rested on one of the larger stones, then kneeled on the ground. This bottle was one of the many items that hermit crabs get trapped in, so he picked it up and turned it upside down, emptying out the sand. With the sand came several live crabs, along with many who had died after getting trapped.

Taylor learned when hermit crabs needed a new shell, they follow the scent of a dead hermit crab to take the vacant shell. If a hermit crab crawls into a bottle looking for food and then is unable to climb back out the curved bottleneck, it will die, and its scent will trick other hermit crabs into the same bottle looking for a new shell, who also get trapped and die.

He knew he could not help all the creatures on the many riverbanks around his home, yet he kept going. For every animal he helped, it meant they had another chance at life. Leaning over to pick up a plastic bag, he shook it out to make sure there wasn't anything hiding inside, and then put it in his trash bag to throw out later. Taylor shook his head in frustration. *If only people would stop littering!*

Holding onto his bike as he got back to his feet, his eye caught the outline of a large box-shaped object hidden in the trees, and there was something moving inside! As he moved towards it, he called out, "Who are you? Are you okay?"

He didn't remember there being any kind of trap or cage here before. The forest that lined the beach, as well as the beach itself, were part of a nature refuge and there was no hunting or trapping allowed. *This trap shouldn't be here!*

Glancing around to make sure there was no one else in the area, he moved a little closer to the cage, calling out softly, "No need to be afraid of me. I'm here to help."

"Who are you? Why can I understand you?" a voice responded.

Whoever was in the cage was standing as far back as possible. The cage measured about three feet high, three feet wide and about six feet deep. The sides and back were covered by leaves and branches leaving only the front bars of the cage visible. *It must have been set up to be hidden until the trap door sprang shut!*

"Please know that I am here to help you," Taylor said. "My friends Knocker and Ituria gave me a special feather that allows me to talk with animals. Do you see a way that I can free you?"

As the trapped animal slowly came to the front of the cage, Taylor recognized that this was one of the few red wolves that remained in North Carolina. At last count, there were only eight wild red wolves in the whole state! Between the developers and short-sighted residents who felt any wolf was a threat, the population had gone from 120 wolves introduced into the nature preserves, to just eight remaining, and the last sightings revealed they were all in this small wildlife refuge living within five to six miles of the river. Although they were now a protected species, some people just didn't care and wanted them all gone!

"Let me help you!" Taylor said. "What can I do to help?"

"I don't know that you can help me; I have tried to get out of this trap, but I cannot." He was scared, and he started pacing back and forth. "What can I do to get away?"

"I'm Taylor," Taylor answered, trying to calm him down. "Don't worry. We'll figure this out. What's your name?" As he waited for an answer, Taylor leaned over the cage and started pulling branches off to see what they were up against. The cage was built with strong metal bars, and they were welded together. The front wall was attached to a long metal spring, and it must have snapped shut when the wolf entered the cage.

"I'm Brandon," came the soft reply as the wolf sat down in the cage. "I have only been in this area for a short time. I am always running from the humans. I thought I might be safe here; I was hungry and smelled some food and went toward it and this trap snapped shut on me."

Moving from the bike and leaning on the cage, Taylor could tell this cage was sturdy and not something he could easily break, or even open. *What can I do? Who can help us?*

"Brandon, know that I will do everything I can to get you out of here, okay?" Taylor said, needing to let the wolf understand that he would not leave him alone.

Remembering that many animals he had talked with before knew of Ituria, he called out to any creature within earshot, "Can anyone help me get in touch with Ituria?"

Then Taylor waited, hoping he would get an answer.

Chapter Two

HELP ARRIVES

"**W**ho seeks assistance from Ituria?" came a wary reply from behind the line of trees. Taylor couldn't identify the owner of the voice and peered through the tree trunks to see who might be responding.

"I am a friend of Ituria and Knocker," Taylor replied, "and I need their assistance to help rescue a wolf trapped in a cage!"

"Are you a human?" came the response. The voice was still guarded—the owner didn't want to be seen.

"Yes... I am." Taylor was getting a little worried now. *What can I say to make whoever is responding understand?* Most animals feared humans and would do all they could to stay away from them. He didn't blame them, but he needed help now.

"I am part of Ituria's Alliance and am here to help creatures that are threatened by humans!" He paused for a moment, and hearing no response, continued. "I need to rescue the wolf caught in this trap before the poachers find him. Can you help me?"

"Are you … Taylor?" the voice said softly, still questioning whether it should reveal itself.

"Yes." Taylor replied as he reached for his bike and started to back away from the cage. Maybe this was a human responding. *But how would they know my name?*

Suddenly, a girl appeared from the woods; he could only stare at her as she walked slowly toward him. Taylor had never seen anyone like her before. Tall and slender, she was wearing a knee-length red dress. Her long, grey hair was braided and hanging down the left side, almost to her waist, and she wore boots that came up to her knees. A small satchel with a strap crossed over one shoulder and rested on her right side.

"I will help you free the wolf, Taylor," she said when she was standing in front of him.

"Have you just moved here? I don't remember ever seeing you before." Now it was Taylor's turn to ask questions.

"I am on a mission for Knocker, and he told me the only human I could talk to was Taylor. Are you that Taylor?" She looked at him closely, but he just stared back. It was a standoff, neither was sure if they could trust the other at this point.

Suddenly, the noise from a large engine of a vehicle heading down the dirt road on the other side of the tree line forced the issue. Taylor's head turned toward the sounds as they got closer. There was no more time to discuss. They needed to act!

"Yes, I am that Taylor, Knocker's friend. I need

you to help me open the cage and get the wolf out before the poachers get here. That may be them now," Taylor whispered urgently; deciding that at least for now, he would have to trust her, as he could not get the cage open on his own.

"If you are my Taylor, I will help open the cage," she replied as she walked towards the cage where Brandon was peeking out between the bars. She nodded at Brandon, and he nodded back to her, but neither spoke to the other. Then she looked over to Taylor. "Once he is free, is there a place where the three of us can hide from these poachers you hear coming?"

Thinking for just a moment, Taylor nodded. "Yes! I know of a small cave that we can go to, but we must hurry!"

Reaching the cage, the girl put her hands on the two middle bars on the front of the cage. Gripping the bars tightly, she quickly pulled on them and bent the bars until she cleared a space about ten inches wide, more than wide enough for Brandon to escape.

"Can you get out now?" she asked.

Jumping through the opening created by the girl, Brandon exclaimed, "Yes! Let's get out of here!"

"Human Taylor, you must lead the way!" she called out, waiting for him to show them where to hide. "Brandon, you must follow Taylor!"

Taylor grabbed the handles of his bike and headed towards the cave. "Just over here, follow me!" Moving as fast as he was able, Taylor led the party to a small cave hidden down the beach on the other side of several large trees.

The entrance was hidden, but Taylor knew where the opening was, and they were all able to get inside before they heard the vehicle stop close to the cage. Several people got out, talking among themselves, and they could hear the vehicle doors slam shut. At first, the voices were not loud enough for Taylor to understand them. However, once the people realized their prize was gone, they started getting louder, and Taylor could hear them clearly.

"What happened?" yelled one of them. "Look at the cage! It's busted!"

"Mitch," another yelled. "What could have pried open the bars like that?"

"Look, there are footprints leading away, and there are wolf prints also!" shouted Mitch. "Let's track them down!"

Taylor looked back at the girl and Brandon. "They are coming this way, following our footprints!" he whispered anxiously. "What can we do?" *We didn't have time when escaping to cover our footprints in the sand and now the poachers are after us!*

The girl stepped to the front of the cave and looked back at Taylor and Brandon. "No need to worry. I will handle this. You must stay hidden, no matter what happens, understand?"

Taylor and Brandon nodded. Taylor remembered how she was able to bend the metal bars and hoped she had a plan; he couldn't think of anything at this point.

Not showing a bit of fear, the girl stepped out and started heading up the beach to confront the poachers.

Chapter Three

THE BROKEN TRAP

"Hey, what are you doing on this beach, little girl?" shouted Mitch, who was still angry at seeing his trap broken. They were about fifty feet away from her and heading her way. "Do you know what happened to our trap back there? Looks like someone busted it up. Do you know anything about that?"

She looked at him but did not respond to his questions; she just kept walking toward them. When she got about ten feet away from them, she stopped and asked, "What are you doing on this beach? No hunting is allowed, you know."

"Who says we're hunting?" Mitch said sarcastically. "We're trapping dangerous animals to protect the people! Now, do you know what happened to our trap?"

"Trapping is still hunting, and no, I don't," she replied in a matter-of-fact tone.

"Well, what are you doing here?" Mitch asked. "This isn't a place for little girls! You need to run home now, okay?"

"No, I don't think so. I'm here enjoying the beach," she continued in a calm voice. "My brother and his dog were here earlier, but they went home. At least he said they were headed home."

Looking at the footprints in the sand, she continued. "Is that what you were looking at? My brother and his dog's footprints? They have already gone. I decided to stay a bit longer and watch the little crabs; they are so cute!" She reached down and picked up a small hermit crab and smiled at it.

"We want to know who broke our trap. Did you see anything?" Mitch replied with a nasty voice. "Is there something you're not telling us?"

"No," she said, shaking her head. "And I thought I already answered that question." She was looking around at the water's edge, not really interested in talking with them. "Anyway, it looked like that when we arrived." The girl continued her walk along the beach, leading the men away from the cave, and the three poachers turned to follow her.

Staying near the edge of the water, she didn't look at or pay any attention to the three men following her, but a quick glance back now and then confirmed they were still behind her, watching what she was doing. Every so often she would bend over to pick up a shell to look at, and then throw it into the water. After about five minutes, when she had gotten them far from the cave, she turned back to look at them.

"Why are you following me? Don't you have somewhere to be?" she asked. "Am I going to have to call my brother back? He won't be too far away yet."

One man stopped walking and turned to the others and asked, "Mitch, why don't we just fix up the trap and set it again?"

"Yes, that's probably best," Mitch said in an irritated voice, still staring at the girl, wondering how she fit into this. "I'm still wondering what type of machine or device they used to pry open the bars."

"I don't really know. I will go find my brother and his dog now." Leaving the water's edge and heading back to the trees, the girl walked until she got to the edge of the trees, getting a little closer to the cage. When she got closer to the cage she looked inside and then looked back at the men, who were following her again. "Why do you trap things in this cage? Why would you do such a mean thing?"

"Oh, they're just animals, and we're paid a lot of money to get rid of them!" Mitch answered with a smirk. "We should have them all cleared out by the weekend."

That was not the right answer! The girl glared at Mitch, her eyebrows furrowed, jaw clenched, and lips pressed tightly together, while she tried to control her contempt for these men, who cared nothing about killing animals as long as they got paid enough.

"Gentlemen!" she shouted as she turned to face them. "As I said before, trapping is still hunting, so my suggestion is that you take that metal box and leave the area—now!" She pointed to the cage and then to their vehicle. "This needs to go! This is a nature refuge, and you are not allowed to hurt the animals here; do you understand?" Her anger was almost at the boiling point. "This is your last warning!" Standing with her hands on her hips, she glared at them, waiting for their response.

Two of the men stepped back, astonished by this new attitude, but Mitch wasn't afraid. He stood his ground and challenged her. "What gives you the right to tell me what to do? Huh?"

"I have right on my side, so I will win. What do you have?" she countered.

"Well, right doesn't always win, does it?" Mitch answered in a menacing tone. "Let's see who wins this one. I'm not leaving. You guys, you stay here too. We're not going to let a little girl tell us what to do!"

"So be it!" the girl answered. "You have been warned!"

Stepping over to the large cage, she grabbed the two sides and picked it up, holding it over her head for just a second as she glared at Mitch, then she threw it into the road about fifty feet away. Landing with a loud crash, the sides of the cage were smashed, the bars bent and cracked. Looking back at Mitch, she asked, "Now what are you going to do?"

"Mitch," shouted one of the others, "that cage weighs over a hundred pounds! How did she do that?"

"Oh, that was just some kind of trick—she must have used a rope or something," Mitch mumbled in a subdued tone; he wasn't so sure any more about what was going on.

"Alright, little lady," he called out to her. "We'll leave for now, but we will be back. Don't you worry about that. I suggest that you not be here when we get back, understand?"

"I will be where I want to be!" she shouted back, then she silently watched as the men grabbed the broken pieces of the cage and loaded it into the back of their vehicle.

She knew the fight wasn't over yet by a long shot. However, she needed to get back to Taylor and Brandon.

Chapter Four

IDENTITIES REVEALED

Waiting until the men got into their vehicle and drove away before making any movement, she ran back to the cave. Once inside, she whispered, "Are you okay, Taylor and Brandon?"

"Yes," Taylor said, "we are fine. Thank you so much for coming to Brandon's rescue. If you hadn't been here, they would have taken him away, maybe even shot him."

"Yes, Megan, thank you for helping me get out of the cage," Brandon added with appreciation. "We were very lucky that you were around."

"Taylor, how do you have the power to talk and understand the animals? I was watching you as you were talking to Brandon. I don't understand. Please explain." Megan looked at Taylor and waited for his response.

"Well, when Knocker was here about a year ago, I was able to help him rescue a family of red wolves and transport them to the moon so they could be safe," Taylor paused as he pulled out a necklace that he was wearing. It was attached to a feather that was enclosed in a hard plastic shell. "See, this feather was knocked off of me by a hunter when I was a hawk, and Ituria told me as long as I had it with me, I could talk to the local animals."

"Taylor, now I understand," Megan said, nodding her head. "And if Ituria provided you with a magic feather, then it is magic indeed! Although we may need to talk later of how you became a hawk, that still does not make sense."

"Please allow me to introduce myself," Megan continued, as she stood up straight. "I am Megan, and I am a friend of Knocker and Ituria also. Knocker rescued me and has allowed me to help him on some of his missions." Then she gracefully bowed to Taylor and Brandon.

"This is my first mission alone," Megan added as her voice trembled, showing she was a little nervous. "Knocker said that if I needed help, I could only talk to a human named Taylor, so I'm glad that I found you. Brandon and I were discussing how to get him out of the cage when you came onto the beach, that is why I was hiding in the trees," Megan explained. "We could not understand how you, a human, were able to talk to Brandon."

"What is your mission for Knocker?" Taylor asked. "Is there anything I can do to help?"

"Well," Megan began, "we have known for a several weeks that there is a band of poachers hunting and trapping the red wolves. We may have just met the leader, Mitch, who is out to make as much money as he can by trapping and killing the few red wolves remaining.

"Knocker has asked me to come to this area and defend the wolves—and to cause these poachers as much trouble as possible—and if needed, we will take the remaining wolves back to Ituria's Island rather than let them be killed."

Looking directly at Taylor, she continued, "Taylor, I do not know if I should involve any humans in this mission; however, since you have worked with Knocker before, I will talk to Knocker to see if you can assist us without becoming a target of the poachers yourself. That would be my main concern, that they would associate you with me, and then come after you when my mission is completed."

"Brandon," she said as she turned to look at him, "I offer you the choice of going to Ituria's Island now or staying to help me. You would be able to talk to the red wolves without raising suspicion and may be able to help us locate them. I am afraid that if I call out to them, my natural voice would be a beacon to any hunters around the area."

"I will stay and help," Brandon replied quickly. "You are helping save my friends and I am glad to assist you!"

Megan was trying to figure out all the angles to keep Taylor and Brandon safe while continuing her mission. Taylor was following her train of thought; however, he was confused when she mentioned her "natural voice." *What could she mean by that?*

"Megan," Taylor started, then hesitated for a second before continuing, "Megan, what do you mean by your natural voice?"

Megan was not sure how to answer. *How much does Taylor know?*

"Tell me, Taylor," she said in reply, nervousness creeping back into her voice. "How did you come to meet Knocker? Have you ever heard his natural voice?"

"Yes … I have," Taylor said slowly. He looked closely at Megan and asked, "Are you related to Knocker?"

"When I am not in this form, I am the same type of being as Knocker. I have taken this form to try and blend in with the humans."

"Got it!" Taylor exclaimed, remembering when he first saw Knocker in his true form, a fantastically large dragon with blue/green scales and large wings. "No further explanation is necessary. Welcome, Megan, please know I will do all in my power to help your mission succeed!"

"Thank you, Taylor, I appreciate it," she replied, relieved that Taylor understood. "Maybe we can work out a plan to get these poachers out of here for good! You, Brandon, and I—we would make a great team!"

Chapter Five

PLANS ARE MADE

"Okay, Taylor, please understand that my top priority is to make sure that the poachers do not connect you with my mission. I have been causing problems with their camp and their traps for a few days now. You must realize that once Brandon and I leave, if they have seen you with me, they may seek revenge against you." Megan spoke quickly and her voice was stressed, she needed to make sure she didn't put Taylor in danger by allowing him to assist.

"Please let me know what your normal daily schedule is, so we may work around it. Also, where do you live? How far away from this beach? I have located the poacher's camp, and it is a few miles to the west."

Megan added, "One more thing you need to know: I have had very little contact with humans for more than three hundred years, and I will need you to assist so I do not act in a way that is not human when I am in this form."

"Well, I live a few miles south of here. It will take a while to get there, as I'll need to walk with the bike here." Taylor paused, thinking to himself, and then asked, "What did Knocker tell you about me?"

Looking at Taylor with a questioning gaze, Megan replied, "Well, before I came here, Knocker told me that you were the only human I should talk to, and I could not trust anyone else. He said you were a very brave and courageous human, putting the animals you were rescuing before yourself, and I could trust you with my secret identity. Is there something else I should know?"

"Yes," Taylor answered a little hesitantly. "It sounds like Knocker did not tell you that I have difficulty walking without help. I usually use this bike to walk for balance, and I cannot walk without something to hold onto. Knocker did not see this as a bad thing, and he provided me with a magic potion to transform into a hawk to show him where the wolves were trapped."

Looking away, not wanting to see the normal response when he revealed his physical challenges, he continued quietly, "I hope you will still let me help in your mission, even with my physical limitations."

"Taylor! Of course, I do want and need your help!" exclaimed Megan with a smile. "Yes, Knocker said that movement was not one of your greatest attributes, but that your courage and spirit more than compensated for any difficulty in your mobility. He did say that we would need to work around it and be mindful, since everyone has different strengths and weaknesses."

Looking back at Megan, Taylor's face lit up with a big smile. *Knocker did understand!*

"And just so you know, Taylor, my main weakness is that I have difficulty at being able to control my temper," Megan said with a chuckle. "If you see me ready to blow my top, please tell me to calm down, okay? I have learned that I must remain calm, or I could transform back into a dragon, which would not be a good thing for anyone."

"You bet!" replied Taylor with a grin. "That's a deal!"

"Taylor," she said, "One of your strengths is that you are the only one here who will understand what these other humans are saying. If we can get you close enough, you will need to be our ears, to let us know what they are planning so we can react accordingly."

"I have a translation stone," she continued, taking a small flat stone out of her bag to show him. "But it only works for about 10 feet. Your magic feather has no limits as to distance; non-humans will understand you no matter how far away you are from them. You can also understand what the poachers are saying and relay it to us, so your help will be invaluable."

Taylor nodded, understanding that he really did have an important role in the mission.

"And Brandon," Megan said, "You are one of only a few red wolves left in this area. As I noted before, my mission can proceed in one of two ways: the first is to keep you and the other red wolves from being killed by these poachers, or second—to gather all of you together and take you to the moon where you will be safe!"

"I understand and I am glad you are here, Megan," Brandon replied, but his voice was very serious. "At this point, however, I don't know if you will be able to get rid of the poachers. And if you can get rid of these, there will always be someone willing to take their place. So maybe we should work on gathering the remaining red wolves and removing them from this area before we are all trapped by the poachers."

"Do you know where the others are?" Megan asked.

"I know where two are, Peter and Indy; we will have to search for the others. We have all been hiding from humans for so long, I have not been able to keep track of where the others are hiding," Brandon replied. "Our first stop should be at the poachers' camp. I have seen it also, and there is one wolf there now. It appears they are keeping it alive so that they cannot be accused of killing it if they are found by the authorities. That's why they are using cage traps now, rather than poisoned food or clamp traps like they had used previously."

"That sounds like a great first step, to rescue the one that has already been captured," Megan agreed. "And while we are there, maybe we can see who and what we are up against."

"Brandon," Megan continued, "can you please stay with Taylor, and lead him to just outside the camp—don't go in—stay hidden. I will go ahead and survey the situation. Taylor, is there any time limitation that we should be aware of? Do you need to be home at a certain time to avoid suspicion with your family?"

"My mom knows that I come over to the beach after school and her only rule is that I get home before dark." Taylor looked at his watch and added, "It looks like it will be getting dark in about four hours, so I will need to be back home by then. Will that give us enough time?"

"We will make sure you are home by dark!" Megan answered and started out toward the poacher's camp, with Brandon and Taylor following behind her.

Chapter Six

RANDALL'S RESCUE

As Taylor and Brandon approached the poacher's camp, they paused to look around. Megan had gone before them, but she was nowhere to be seen.

Pointing to a large bush that would protect them from view of the poachers, Taylor whispered, "Let's hide behind here. I can hear what they are saying, but they won't be able to see us."

Brandon nodded his head and went behind the bush, crouching down to be as small as possible. Taylor rolled the bike behind Brandon and carefully laid it down on its side. Then he moved closer to Brandon on his hands and knees.

"Let's just listen. I will be able to understand the conversation; we need to know what they are doing."

Taylor raised his head to look through the bushes, trying to get a mental picture of the camp. The west side had three tents set up. Two of the tents had flaps on all sides, but the third one—the one farthest away to the south—only had a canvas top. The sides had been rolled up and tied and underneath the tent there was a large table with chairs. *It looks like this is where the poachers meet to have meals and plan their activities.*

There was a middle walkway about six feet across, and the east side had one large tent that looked like a combination of a supply tent and kitchen. Two of the canvas sides were tied up, and Taylor could see a cooking stove and several of shelves with supplies and food. On each side of this tent, Taylor could see the large trap cages piled on top of each other. Some were folded down, and others were assembled, just like the cage they had seen on the beach. Looking closer at the assembled cages, he could see that one of them had a wolf in it. He couldn't tell if it was alive or not though, as it was laying down and its eyes were closed.

Brandon nudged Taylor with his snout, getting his attention, as voices were heard coming out of one of the tents. Taylor ducked back down, close to the ground so he would be hidden by the bushes and listened for any conversation that might come their way.

"I'm telling you, Roy," the voice started as two men walked out of the middle tent on the left. "When I saw that little girl throw that cage, I was ready to pack up and get out. Things are getting a little weird around here. All those weird accidents over the past couple of days, things breaking and disappearing."

"You know Mitch won't like it if you leave, Bill, don't you?" Roy replied.

"I know, I know," Bill answered. "We signed on to stay until we remove all the wolves from the area, and we're getting paid good money to get rid of these critters by the developer, too! More than I would normally make in a year!"

"I know. The money is great!" Glancing over at the wolf laying in the cage next to the supply tent, Roy continued, a bit less enthusiastic. "But look at that little one in the cage. What did he do wrong to deserve being locked up and killed?" As he walked into the supply tent, he said quietly to Bill, "Maybe we should feed it something, or at least give it some water, huh?"

"I'm not sticking my hand in there," Bill argued. "You do what you want."

"Well, I will," Roy said, just a little defiant of the orders they had been given. "It's just plain mean to leave it in that cage without giving it any water at least." Picking up a small bowl, Roy poured some water from the jug until it was about half-full. Then he looked over at the cage, "Yep, this will work," he said to himself.

Walking over to the front of the cage, he slowly slid it between the bars. "Hey, little buddy. Here's some water!" he called out in a friendly voice once his hands were away from the cage.

"Okay, enough of this, Roy," Bill replied harshly, not wanting to give in to his emotions as Roy had. They couldn't have any compassion for these animals, or they might not complete their job of ridding the forest of all the red wolves, and that was what they were being paid for!

"Mitch will be waiting for us up on the road, working on the broken cage. He should be back with the parts by now. We have to get back and help, okay?" Bill urged as he turned to head east. "You know we'll hear about it if Mitch sees us doing anything for those critters."

"I know," Roy replied in a disheartened voice as he took a quick glance back at the wolf in the cage, who had not moved yet.

"I'm coming. I'm coming!" he called to Bill and caught up with him as they left the camp heading east towards the dirt road that runs along the beach to meet up with Mitch.

Waiting a minute to make sure they were gone, Taylor and Brandon quietly got up and entered the camp, going quickly over to the cage with the wolf inside. Taylor laid the bike against the cage and braced himself on the top bars of the cage, looking down at the wolf inside.

"Can you hear me?" whispered Taylor. "I'm here to help you."

The wolf moved for the first time, slowly lifting its head, and looked in Taylor's direction.

"Can you get up? We are going to get you out of the cage," Taylor said. "Try and drink some of that water in the bowl. It should be okay. It came from the same jug the humans drank from."

"I will try," came the weak response. "I don't know if I can move too fast though."

Suddenly footsteps could be heard coming from the woods near north entrance. Taylor quickly turned and looked behind him, worried that the poachers were returning. However, it was Megan who was running toward them, realizing that there was little time left for this one.

"Let me get him out of here and take him back to Ituria. They will help him!" she whispered urgently as she moved in front of Taylor and swiftly busted the front gate off the cage at the hinges. Crawling into the cage, she lifted the wolf in her arms and whispered gently, "Hold on just a bit longer, little one. We will get you to a better home and get you well again!"

As she crawled out of the cage with the wolf in her arms, she whispered, "Human Taylor and Brandon, I must take this one back now!" Running quickly to a clearing, she looked up at the sky, searching for something. "There it is!" she called out as she focused on one spot in the sky. "I can see it!"

"Guardian, I need help now!" Megan called to the sky. Even though it was still afternoon, the moon was already visible in the sky to the east—and it looked like Megan was calling to it! *Can someone hear her from the moon?*

"Taylor!" she cried out. "You must keep Brandon safe!"

Suddenly, a blue flash of light enveloped Megan and then she and the sick wolf were gone.

Chapter Seven

TRIP TO
TAYLOR'S HOUSE

With the sudden disappearance of Megan, Taylor realized that he needed to get Brandon away from the poacher's camp.

"Brandon," he whispered. "Let's go to my house, and you can hide in my back yard. The poachers won't go there, okay?"

Brandon nodded, agreeing to Taylor's plan, looking around to make sure no one would see them as they left. "Yes, I will stay with you. I know the area where your home is, and there are two of my friends living over in that area, Peter and Indy. If we can find them, they can join us."

"Agreed!" Taylor whispered. "Mitch said he was going to get rid of all the wolves in this area by the weekend—that's only two days from now—so I do not think that staying here is going to be the final choice of Megan's mission." Taylor's voice became soft and sad as he spoke the words that they both knew were true. "Unfortunately, there is no safe place for you or the other wolves here anymore."

Brandon's head dropped as he realized that there was no way he could remain here. "I guess the poachers have won," he said sadly.

"No, they haven't!" Taylor replied emphatically. "Not as long as there are people willing to fight for the animals—like me!" He reached out and put his hand on Brandon's shoulder as he continued, trying to comfort him. "Look, if you go to the moon with Megan for a while, maybe things will get better here and maybe you can come back!"

Heading toward the beach, Taylor knew how to get home from there. Because he was walking with his bike, he figured it would take about an hour and a half to get home—half an hour to get back to the beach and another hour to walk the two miles to his house.

"What we'll need to do is to make a plan to locate where the other wolves are," Taylor said as they got to the dirt road that ran from the beach to his house. "Earlier you said you know where two of them are hiding. Once we get them, maybe they will know where the others are, and perhaps we can ask the animals around here if they know also."

Taylor paused a minute to think. "Last official count there were only eight wolves left—that includes you, the one Megan rescued, Peter and Indy—we need to find the other four! Does that sound right to you?"

"Yes, that sounds right," Brandon replied and nodded in agreement as he and Taylor started walking again. "And hopefully Megan will join us once she gets back. She will be able to ask the local animals which way we went, so she will be able to find us."

After reaching the beach, Taylor took the lead and headed towards his house. They had been walking for about forty-five minutes when Brandon sniffed the air and stopped.

"Taylor," he said softly, "Peter and Indy may be close. If you stand here for a minute, I will go check."

"Okay, Brandon, but please don't get out of sight! We don't know what the poachers have been doing since we left their camp!" Taylor was worried, knowing that they were not safe until they got back to his house.

Taylor watched as Brandon ran a few hundred feet into a field, and then heard some low growling and barking as Brandon was talking to another wolf. He listened as Brandon told the other wolf what had happened. Soon Brandon was heading back, being followed by two other wolves.

"Taylor," Brandon called in a low growl, "this is Peter and Indy. They have been hiding in this area, trying to avoid the humans who have been hunting in the area for the past few days. They have asked if they can join us to escape the hunters."

"Of course!" Taylor answered, keeping his voice low. "I'm Taylor; glad to meet you, Peter and Indy. Please stay with us and we will make sure you get to a safe place where there are no humans hunting you.

Let's go to my house first, so we can discuss how to gather the others."

"Brandon, you are right. He really can talk to us!" Peter replied in a surprised voice but also keeping his voice low so that it would not carry and reveal their location.

"Taylor, thank you for rescuing us! For the first time in a while, I don't feel as though any second someone is going to shoot me and my little brother, Indy. Since my mom and dad were killed by hunters when Indy was a pup, I've been taking care of him." Peter turned his head and motioned the other wolf forward. "Please meet Indy, my brother and best friend."

"Hi, human Taylor," Indy said softly. "How can you keep us safe? And how can you talk to us?"

"Let's get back to my house first and then we can discuss it all. We are vulnerable out here." Taylor started walking again, looking around to make sure no one was watching them, and going as quickly as he could towards his house.

As they entered the front yard of his house, Taylor called out to his mom, "Hi, Mom! I'm home now. I'm going to stay outside for a while and watch my little animal friends, okay?"

Taylor pointed at some hedges and motioned for the wolves to hide behind them.

"Hi, Taylor. Of course!" his mom replied from inside the house. "Remember, I have to go to work tonight. I'll be leaving in a few minutes and getting home around midnight. Make sure you get inside when it gets dark. There's some dinner in the fridge."

"Thanks, mom! I'll be sure to go inside by dark!" Taylor used his bike to walk to the back yard, leaned the bike up against the shed, and sat in a lawn chair nearby. He would sit here until his mom left. He nodded to the wolves hiding in the bushes and wondered what would happen next.

Chapter Eight

CURRENT SITUATION

Taylor waved to his mom as she drove away from the house. Once she was out of sight, he motioned for the wolves to come join him.

"Hey guys, let me go see what we have to eat in the house. I'll be right back." Taylor got up and walked to the back door, using the handrail his mom put in so he could go out into the yard by himself when he wanted to get outside. He came out a few minutes later with a plate of macaroni and cheese. "Let me know if you like this, okay?"

As he was placing the plate on the ground, Taylor saw Megan in the distance, looking around, heading in their general direction. Waving to her, he called out, "Over here in the back!"

Peter and Indy looked up and saw a human heading their way. Indy quickly ran behind Peter, and Peter took a protective stance in front of him, wondering why Taylor would welcome a human when they were so vulnerable. Sniffing several times, Peter was also puzzled at the smell.

"Taylor," he whispered, "Who is this? Is she safe? She has a smell I have not come across before—she is not human!"

"It's okay, Peter," Taylor replied to reassure him. "She is a friend!"

"Taylor, so glad I found you!" Megan exclaimed as she walked into the back yard. Seeing two more wolves, she asked, "Did you and Brandon find some other wolves? Great work!"

"Greetings to you, new friends!" Megan called to Peter and Indy. "I am Megan. I am here to help protect you!"

"I'm glad you're back, Megan," Taylor said with a smile. Then his voice turned serious, concerned for the little wolf. "How is the little wolf you rescued earlier? Is he better now?"

"Yes," Megan replied, nodding her head. "Guardian had summoned Simon, one of Ituria's healers, and he was waiting for us when we arrived. Within an hour of initial treatment, the young wolf was able to sit up and move again." Her voice got angry as she continued, "It appears that the poachers did not give him any food or water, so he was very dehydrated and weak."

"His name is Randall. He was caught in the trap a few days ago and asked me to thank all who helped rescue him, so I convey to you and Brandon his sincere thanks! Once he was safe, I returned here."

Indy's curiosity overcame his fear, and he came out from behind Peter, walking over until he was close to Megan. "Hi, I'm Indy. Where do you live?"

"Hi Indy. I'm Megan, and I live on Ituria's Island." Megan smiled and knelt on one knee so she could look directly at Indy. "I'm working with Taylor and Brandon to try and rescue the remaining red wolves in the area and take them to a place safe from hunters and guns. Would you like to come live with me?"

Now it was Peter's turn to be cautious. He needed to know more before he would agree to go with her anywhere. "Megan, I am Peter, Indy's older brother. You do not smell like a human, but you look like one. Who are you? I need to know more before I can make any decisions on where Indy and I go." Peter was still concerned with the confusing signals he was getting from her; he did not trust her yet.

Megan sat on the ground between Peter and Indy, so they could talk face to face.

"Peter, you are correct that I am not a human. But I am in this form for a reason. If I was here in my real form, I would be hunted by all the humans in the area, which would defeat my mission of rescuing you, Indy, Brandon, and the others of your kind that are being unfairly hunted."

Megan looked at Peter, wondering if he had any other questions. "Does that help any?"

"Yes, it helps a little," Peter replied, still wondering what kind of creature she was. "Brandon, have you seen Megan in her true form? Do you trust her?"

"Peter, I have not seen Megan in her true form, but know that she is here to help us, and she lives on Ituria's Island. Just like Taylor here, she is part of Ituria's Alliance, sent here to help and protect animals from cruelty at the hands of humans." Brandon walked over and sat down next to Megan. "She res-cued me from a trap earlier today, and I trust her to do what is best for us."

"Megan," Brandon continued. "We need to gather the remaining four wolves still in this wild-life refuge and get everyone out of here immediately. Do you have any idea how to find them?"

"I agree with Brandon, Megan," Taylor added. "The poachers said they would have everyone trapped within the next two days. They must know where the remaining four are, even if we do not. What can we do?"

"Peter," Megan asked, "do you know where the other four wolves could be? Randall said he knew of four wolves that were staying together as a pack so they could take turns watching out for the poachers. Randall said the four were Francie and Silvia—two adult wolves—and Sally and Rebecca, who are less than a year old."

"I remember where they are, or at least the last place I saw them," Peter responded. "There is a small stream a little farther south and west. We saw them a few days ago, Indy and me. The adults were teaching the pups how to catch crabs and fish in the stream. The stream empties into the river to the east. We joined them so Indy could learn too, right Indy?" Peter turned to Indy and smiled as he remembered the activities of that day.

"Yes!" Indy replied. "That was fun to catch the little fish—they were delicious!"

"Okay, we should head in that direction now," Megan said. "Taylor, do you want to remain here or go with us? How much time do you have before you must be inside with your mother?"

"My mom is working tonight, so I can probably stay out a little later if …" Taylor started, but he was drowned out by a loud voice screeching overhead.

"Megan! The poachers have trapped some more wolves!" came a cry from the sky. "You must hurry!"

Chapter Nine

MEGAN TO THE RESCUE

"Taylor, I have to go now!" Megan called as she quickly stood up. "I had some friends watching the poachers. They were to tell me if the poachers have caught any wolves—that's who is calling out to me now."

"What should we do?" Taylor called to her as she started running away.

"Keep the others safe and together!" Megan called back. "We must be ready to leave at a moment's notice, once we have everyone gathered together!"

"Okay, I will!" Taylor replied as Megan disappeared into the woods. He gathered the three wolves around him. "Where can you go that you will be safe? Do you think we should stay here?"

"I haven't seen the poachers go into human areas. When I see them, they always stay in the forest. Possibly because we are afraid to go near humans, so they figure we won't be around humans," Brandon replied. "It may be better to stay here until Megan returns."

"Then we will stay here," Taylor replied. "Does that work for you and Indy, Peter?"

"I agree we should stay here," Peter responded. "However, will our new friend, Megan, be okay by herself against the poachers?"

Taylor thought for a moment. His first thought was, *Of course she will be okay—she is a dragon!* But then he remembered that she is a dragon in the form of a human—*Will that make any difference?*

"I don't know if she will be okay," Taylor said in a worried voice. Turning and calling into the sky, he called out, "Friends of Megan, let me know if she needs help, please! She is not familiar with how humans work and think! She may not know how to respond to protect herself and the wolves! We must keep her calm and not react to challenges by the poachers!"

A large hawk flew down onto a branch near Taylor. "I will find her and watch, and if she is in need of help, I will come back and find you!" The hawk then took off, heading to the west where Megan had disappeared into the woods.

"Thank you!" Taylor called out as he watched it fly away.

"Okay," Taylor said to the wolves. "Maybe we can set up some type of relay so that we will know what Megan is doing. And if I need to go after her, I want you all to stay here behind the house. You should not leave. We will meet you back here, okay?"

"But what about you?" Peter said. "Will you be able to protect her?"

"It's not so much as protect her, but to keep her from doing something that will get the poachers after her that I am worried about," Taylor replied, thinking back to her last interaction with the poachers, where her temper quickly rose when challenged. If she were to lose control of her emotions, she could reveal her true form!

"Are there any other friends of Megan that can help us?" Taylor called out.

Several smaller birds of various types came down to land next to Taylor and the wolves, chirping loudly as they talked to each other.

A cardinal hopped over to Taylor and said, "We will start a line following Megan, so we can relay back and forth what is going on and keep you informed of what is happening."

"That would be great!" Taylor replied. "Please do this as soon as possible, as I am worried about Megan."

The birds flew up into the sky, going in the same direction as Megan, and Taylor watched as the first stopped in a tree in front of his house while the others kept flying toward Megan. The cardinal called down to Taylor, "We will relay the current situation every few minutes to you. And if you are needed, you will be able to follow the relay line to Megan!"

"Thank you, friend!" Taylor called out. *At least I can keep track of what is going on.*

Looking back at his new wolf friends, he continued, "If for any reason I need to go help Megan, go into the shed here and be totally quiet. If the poachers do show up, they should not go into another human's property or buildings. That is the only safe place I can think of. I am worried that they may come back this way." Taylor's voice was low and concerned. He needed to keep these wolves safe, but what could he do if the poachers showed up?

"Taylor," Brandon asked quietly. "If you need to help Megan, shouldn't we go with you?"

"Yes, that might be better," Peter added, agreeing with Brandon. "We will still all be together, and the birds can relay to Megan where we are. I do not feel safe near any human dwellings, and I must do what is best for Indy."

"That may be the better plan, guys," Taylor agreed. "I would always appreciate your help. But we must make plans on how to respond if we need to set out after Megan. We all have strengths and weaknesses, so working together is the best idea."

Sitting in a circle and talking quietly, Taylor and the wolves discussed what would happen if the call came that Megan needed them. For several minutes, they reviewed various scenarios and how they should react. Their discussions were cut short by a call from the tree.

"Megan needs your help!" the cardinal called out. "She went to rescue the other wolves, and now they are all trapped!"

Taylor stood up and grabbed his bike, immediately heading toward the path Megan took. "To all my friends in the forest, please let me know what you see! What is going on? We will need to work together to get them away from the poachers! The other humans will not understand you, but I will. Please, let me know what is going on!"

Brandon, Peter, and Indy joined Taylor, following behind him and keeping a lookout in all directions. Although they were not sure exactly what they were up against or what they could do, they knew that they were needed, and time was of the essence.

Chapter Ten

FINDING MEGAN

Taylor and the wolves went quickly along the dirt path, encouraged by the constant chirping of birds who were in the trees telling him which direction to go.

"Taylor, she turned south here, and then went around the stream!" called out a blue jay. Taylor followed its directions and altered his track accordingly.

"Make sure we are searching for any humans in the area. It is important we know where they are and what they are doing!" Taylor called out.

"You are not too far now. Caution is needed," said the hawk Taylor had seen earlier as he flew down and landed on the handlebars of Taylor's bike.

"Agreed!" Taylor whispered to the hawk. "I will not speak further, but please keep informing me of where Megan and the other wolves are, and which way I need to go, please!"

"Taylor, friend of Megan," it responded, "I am Michael; I will stay just above you and let you know what is going on. I looked where they are now, and they appear to be in a large pit with a net stretched over the top. You are not very far now!" Then the hawk took off and flew above Taylor as they got closed to the poachers.

Taylor nodded his head to Michael. Looking back to the three wolves with him, he whispered urgently, "Remember what we discussed earlier: no matter what, you are not to be seen!" Then he motioned for them to vanish into the underbrush, as he continued walking forward. Soon he could hear some clanking noises and voices in front of him. *I must be close!*

Once he got to the south side of the stream, he could see three men unfolding metal cages and clicking them together, and across from them was a pit with a rope net covering it. He walked a little closer and looked in the pit.

There he saw Megan. She was holding one of the smaller wolves in her arms. The others were all sitting next to her; their eyes were wide, looking around, afraid of what might happen to them. Taylor thought Megan might be whispering to them, but he was not sure. If she spoke loud enough for Taylor to hear, then the poachers would hear her voice also, and it would not be a human voice.

As Taylor got within a few feet of the pit, one of the men looked up and saw him. "Hey, Mitch!" he called out in an irritated voice. "Looks like we got some more company!"

"Oh, hi!" Taylor called out, trying to sound calm. "I'm just passing through on my way home from school." Now walking with his bike directly over to the pit, he exclaimed, "What are you doing? Hey, there's a girl down there with some animals!"

"None of your business, kid!" Mitch replied with a nasty voice. "You just need to keep on walking, okay?"

"But what are you doing?" Taylor repeated, a little louder.

"We're just ridding the forest of some varmints, orders from our boss—it's been cleared!"

"Isn't this a nature refuge? Why are you allowed to hunt here? Why is the girl down there?" Taylor was letting them know he wasn't going to just walk away.

Knowing Megan couldn't talk because she was more than ten feet away from the poachers, he wanted to communicate to her somehow. *What can I say?*

"Hey, down there!" he called out. "Why don't you come join me and get out of the pit?"

Megan looked at Taylor as she shook her head no; she wasn't getting out of the pit.

"Okay," Taylor continued. "Do you want me to go get my mom?"

Before Megan could respond, Mitch yelled at Taylor. "You're not going to get anyone! And if you don't watch out, you will end up in the pit with her!"

Suddenly, a small bird started chirping loudly as it flew above Taylor near the pit. "Taylor," it called out. "The smallest wolf has been hurt and she cannot walk. Megan cannot leave her. What are your plans? What can we do?"

Taylor looked at the men, trying to put a plan in place. The men were about twenty feet away from the pit to his left. He also looked up into the eastern sky and nodded to himself. *We have a chance!* He was going to start removing the net now and hope that the larger birds would see and help.

As he moved his bike closer to the pit, he called out loudly. "I'm going to remove this net; you can't keep this girl and the wolves trapped! Anyone who can hear me, please help me move the net or keep the humans from stopping me!"

"What are you doing?" Mitch called out, turning to run in Taylor's direction, but he was stopped by the smaller birds flying around him, chirping, and pecking at his head and hands. Meanwhile, several larger birds helped Taylor by pulling on the same side of the net he was pulling on. The other two men tried to intervene also, but more birds flew around them, chirping, diving in and out to keep them from getting to Taylor and the larger birds.

Once the net had been pulled from half of the pit, Taylor looked up to the sky and called out as loud as he could, "Guardian, Megan needs help now!"

Taylor fell to the ground as he made one last hard pull, clearing the net from the pit. He hoped his plan worked, as there was no plan B.

Hearing Taylor's yelling, the men stopped and were staring at him, trying to figure out what was going on. What was he trying to do? A few seconds later, a blue flash of light shined on the pit for just a second, and Megan and the wolves were gone.

Now, it was just Taylor and the poachers.

Chapter Eleven

CONFRONTATION

Mitch ran over to Taylor screaming and shaking his fists as he looked in the now empty pit. "What have you done, why did you let them out?"

Reaching over to grab his bike and struggling to stand up, Taylor yelled back. "You have no right to trap animals here and you know it!"

"Look, we get paid by how many wolves we catch, and you just cost me a bundle!" Mitch was standing over Taylor now, glaring at him. "What's got into you?"

"I don't think you should be hunting here. Why don't you just leave?" Taylor replied, still defiant, even though he was totally outnumbered.

"Look, little buddy, my boss wants all the wolves out of here so he can convince the State to let him turn it into a housing development. Now, since you chased those wolves away, you are going to help me catch them again, got it?" Mitch grabbed Taylor by the shoulder and started pulling him toward the other two guys. Taylor held onto his bike and balanced as best he could as he was being pulled forcefully behind Mitch.

"Mitch," Roy said as he watched Mitch pulling Taylor over to them. "This kid ain't going to be any kind of help. Let's just go set up the remaining traps. Bill, why don't you help me set up and bait these traps, okay? We know they are around here somewhere; they didn't just disappear into thin air!"

"I guess you're right. This puny kid isn't worth it. Let's just get the traps set up—we'll have them all by midnight!" Mitch let go of Taylor's shoulder with a quick push, and Taylor fell to the ground.

"Come on, Mitch," Bill asked, even he was appalled by Mitch's actions. "Was that called for? Leave the kid alone."

"How do we know he didn't tell the birds to attack us, huh?" Mitch countered. "Where did all those birds come from? Some were even helping him pull the net off. Did you see that?"

"Hey, Mitch," Roy replied, "listen to yourself. I think the yelling got the birds all riled up."

Walking over to Taylor, Roy helped him to his feet and handed him the bike. "Here, kid. It's time you went home, okay?"

"What are you guys going to do? Are you leaving too?" Taylor asked.

"Kid, if you go now, we'll leave you alone." Roy's voice got a little lower as he continued. "Don't get Mitch any madder, or you may end up in the pit yourself, okay?" Roy's voice conveyed the real danger Taylor faced from Mitch; he was doing his best to convince Taylor to leave.

"Okay," Taylor said. "I'll go now, but you should leave too. You're not welcome here!" Then he turned and headed back towards his house.

"Wait a second, kid!" Mitch yelled. "I thought you were going home from school when you walked over here. Why are you going back the way you came?"

"I came over this way because I heard noises and wanted to see what was going on." Taylor replied, trying to explain away why he was heading east again. "I live a little bit east and south of here."

"Well, you just make sure you get home and stay home, understand?" Mitch said, the threat in his voice was very clear. "If we see you again, you won't get off so easy. Remember that!" Turning to the traps and starting to work on them again, he grumbled to the other two men, "Come on, guys. We got to get the rest of these traps set up—I want to be done with this place!"

Taylor headed back east and walked quickly until he was out of sight of the poachers. It would be getting dark soon, so he needed to make sure the three wolves in his care were still okay. Calling softly into the sky, he said, "Michael, where are the three wolves with me now? Are they okay?"

Michael landed on his shoulder, and he also responded in a low voice, "The three wolves with you are still closer to the poachers than they should be. I will fly over and call them back and tell them stay next to you while still being hidden in the bushes."

"Sounds good, Michael. Thanks! Please tell them to stay hidden and not to get to close to me, especially if I get on one of the roads. We can't trust these guys, okay?" Taylor whispered.

While Taylor kept walking east, he could hear Michael calling to the three wolves hiding in the bushes, telling them to carefully work their way east until they found Taylor, and to always stay hidden. "Taylor says don't let the humans see or hear you for any reason!" was the final call from the hawk.

Without Megan, they were on their own. It had taken over an hour for Megan to return last time, so Taylor figured it could be at least that long before she would be back, if she was even able to return.

"Taylor," Michael called out. "The wolves are near you now."

Nodding, Taylor started talking to himself. "I'm going home now. Just get out of the forest and away from these guys. Mom will have a nice dinner waiting."

"Taylor!" came a screech from the hawk. "They are following you. Wolves stay hidden!"

Taylor nodded again and started walking a little faster. *Should I lead them away from my house? I don't want them to know where I live!*

Wanting to match what he told Mitch before he left, he turned south, away from his house, when he reached a dirt road. Now he was on his own, it was getting dark, and he had nowhere to go!

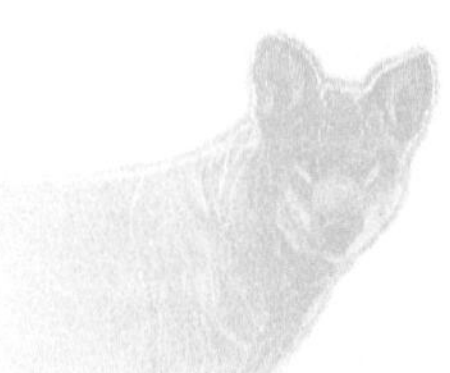

Chapter Twelve

HIDE AND SEEK

Taylor looked to the west, and he could see that the sun would be setting within the next hour. To the east, he could see the moon; it would be a waxing moon tonight and might provide some light once the sun disappeared below the horizon.

Michael kept him updated every minute or two, flying back and forth tracking the poachers and the wolves, and letting Taylor know what was happening.

A loud metallic bang made Taylor jump, and he stopped to figure out where it came from. The bang was quickly followed by loud barking and growling, echoing through the trees to the west of them.

"Mitch!" Roy shouted. "I think we got one of them!"

"Let's get him!" Bill shouted.

Taylor stayed still as he heard the men turn and start running quickly into the forest, they were going to claim their prize. *But I thought there were only eight red wolves? Are there more?*

"Michael, please come here. We need to talk!" Taylor whispered urgently. He hoped all the men had turned back, but he could not count on it. One may have stayed behind to follow him.

"Yes, Taylor! How can I help?" Michael answered as he landed on the seat of Taylor's bike.

"Either the count for red wolves must be wrong, or that was not a red wolf caught in that trap. Can you please have your friends fly throughout this nature refuge and call out to the residents? We need to locate all red wolves that are here." Taylor was anxious, trying to figure out how to locate any other wolves in the area.

"We can't leave anyone; they are in grave danger! Please also put everyone on alert that they are in danger from hunters and that we will update them as we can. Make sure everyone understands about the traps being set, wolves or not, so they don't get caught!" Taylor wanted to make sure no one else was trapped.

"Yes, Taylor, I understand and will get my friends to assist," Michael answered.

"And Michael," Taylor continued with a serious tone, "once you have done that, can you please check on what is trapped in the cage? We will need to plan out another rescue!"

"On my way!" Michael screeched as he took to the sky. Taylor listened as Michael called to all the flying creatures, asking them to spread out and find the locations of any more wolves, to be wary of traps or food laying around, and telling them to report to Taylor any other red wolves they found.

"To my wolf friends," Taylor continued in a whisper, "please stay hidden. If you are near me, let me know, but do not come out of your hiding place."

"Taylor, Indy and I are here to your left, just ahead of you," came a soft growl from in front of him.

"I'm to your right, also just ahead of you," Brandon murmured.

"Taylor," came a small voice from the ground, "you are correct that only two of the humans left. There is one still behind you now. Please be safe."

Looking down, Taylor saw a small rattlesnake on the side of the path looking up at him. "Thank you!" Taylor whispered.

Walking faster as he headed south, he remembered there was a park area that would have streetlights around it. When it got dark, at least he would be able to see what was going on around him and where the third poacher was.

"All my friends, please stay in the wooded area and out of sight!" he whispered. "I am heading to a human area where there will be lights—and maybe other humans."

Approaching the park area, Taylor noted three pavilions with picnic tables. There were light poles on each end and between each of the pavilions.

Looking farther, he saw that there was a group of boys playing soccer on the soccer field beyond the pavilions. The field lights were on. They must have come on to keep the field lit as the sun was setting, allowing the boys to continue their game. *It must be just a practice game. I don't see any referees on the field, and there are no parents sitting in the pavilions.*

Taylor walked over with his bike and sat down at one of the tables near the field, leaning his bike up against the bench where he sat down. He tried to be inconspicuous as he looked back, trying to see who was following him. As he saw a shadow come out of the woods, he quickly turned around and faced the soccer game.

"Well," said Mitch a minute later as he sat down next to Taylor. "Do you mind if I join you?"

"I kind of do. Why are you following me?" Taylor replied, moving a little farther away, pulling the bike a little closer to him, keeping it in between him and Mitch.

"Look," Mitch answered quietly. "You and your shenanigans cost me a lot of money back there. We are going to have to be out all night to make up for lost time, and I want to make sure you won't be going back into the woods again, okay?"

"I'm not going to tell you anything!" Taylor answered, his voice getting louder. One of the coaches looked over his way but didn't say anything.

"Shhh! You don't want to go getting anyone else involved, okay?" Mitch whispered. His voice was turning mean, but he was keeping it low so the people at practice would not hear him.

"Well, maybe I do want to get someone else involved, like Coach Barnes over there!" Taylor was almost yelling now, and the coach turned around again. This time the coach started walking their way.

"You done it now, boy!" Mitch said under his breath. "I'm leaving, but don't let me find you interfering again. Got it?!" He then got up and quickly started walked away, not wanting to have to explain what was going on and why he was harassing Taylor.

"Taylor!" called out Couch Barnes. "Are you okay?"

"Yes, Coach!" Taylor replied. "I'm just going to stay here for a few minutes and then head home. Thanks for checking up on me, I appreciate it!"

"Anytime, son. You are always welcome here!" the coach added. "You'll need to head on home soon, though, because the sun is almost down, and you know it gets dark on the road to your house. No streetlights, remember?"

"Yes, sir!" Taylor said. "I'll just rest here a few minutes first." Taylor needed a few minutes to get his thoughts together, so much had happened, and they were nowhere near being done. As he looked up, he saw a hawk land in one of the trees near him.

"Taylor!" Michael called out. "Yes, it is a red wolf, another yearling who has been hiding out since the rest of his family was killed. He's trapped and will need our help! The poachers are taking the cage back to the camp now!"

Taylor grabbed his bike handles and stood up, ready for the next round with the poachers. *It is going to be a long night!*

Chapter Thirteen

PLANNING ANOTHER RESCUE

Taylor knew he would need a flashlight or lantern, something to help find his way around at night. Even with the moonlight, that would not be enough light for him to get through the woods. Since his house was on the way back to the poacher's camp, he figured he could stop there and grab a flashlight from the shed. There was still enough light to get home, but it would be close. The sun was setting now, and darkness would be here within the hour.

As it got darker, Taylor could see a shadow walking toward him on the road. He wasn't close enough to see anything more than a shadow.

"Taylor!" came a cry from above. It was Michael. "Megan has returned! She is just ahead of you!"

Walking faster, Taylor was soon close enough to talk to her. "Megan, are you okay?"

"Yes, my Taylor," she replied. "Your quick response saved me and the four wolves. The little one had a broken foot and could not walk, so I could not leave them. Thank you!"

"You are welcome, Megan. But we have more worries." Taylor's voice was serious as he stopped walking to explain. "There was another wolf we didn't know about. A small wolf was caught in one of their traps, and he is being taken back to the poacher's camp now."

"The poachers know who I am and are not happy that I helped you and the others escape. They have warned me not to go back into the woods," Taylor continued, talking quickly to make sure Megan was updated. "I have the forest birds searching for any other wolves. We have to make sure we get them all so the poachers don't get them," Taylor paused and then added in a sad voice as he shook his head, "It is no longer safe for them to be here."

"Yes, Taylor, Ituria agrees," Megan said. "We cannot leave them here; it is not safe." Looking around, Megan continued, "Where are the other three: Brandon, Peter, and Indy?" Megan asked, worried that they were not with Taylor.

"They are with me, but I have told them to hide, not to be seen for any reason," Taylor replied. He was talking quickly again, his voice filled with fear. "I am afraid for them. I know the poachers have traps, but I don't know what other weapons they may have, and I am afraid for the wolves!"

"I agree, Taylor. We will give them all a new home. You and the other wolves must remain here—out of sight—until I get back," Megan said. "I will get the little one and bring him back here."

"Brandon, Peter and Indy," Megan continued. "You must be ready to leave on a moment's notice since once the poachers discover what I have done, they will be chasing me. We will only have a minute or two to transport to the moon before they find us." Megan was talking softly, knowing that the wolves were close by and would understand.

"Megan," Taylor responded quietly, offering a different plan, "it may be best if we all stay together. We may have a better chance getting the last wolf freed, and you will have everyone with you to go back to the moon."

"You do have a good point," Megan replied, considering Taylor's suggestion. "It was because I was alone that they were able to trap me with the wolves. Since they have already seen you, we must keep you from being trapped by them, though."

"Agreed. I can get a flashlight from my house, so we can see where we are going," Taylor suggested.

"No, I can see in the dark; I have had a lot of practice." Megan smiled to herself before continuing, "I will lead you; I'll hold onto one of the handles of your bike. The wolves can follow us. The moon will provide enough light for them. I can track the poachers by their smell, and so everyone can just stay with me. Also, we cannot have artificial lights telling them that we are approaching them."

"Megan, there is safety in numbers," Taylor said. "I was wondering if we could get some other of the animals in the area to join us. Many have their own defenses that we can put to good use. I was thinking of the local skunks. Megan, I'm not sure if you know what the skunk's defense is, but it is strong indeed."

Megan looked at Taylor and shook her head, she wasn't familiar with skunks.

"We also have rattlesnakes in the woods, and they can be very frightful to humans also," Taylor continued. "We could call out to the night animals as we make our way to their camp, so we have enough of a force to react to anything they could do. What do you think?"

"That would be a great idea, Taylor! But can we get them all to work together?" Megan asked, not sure how that would work out.

"When you were trapped, I was able to get all the birds in the area to work together, form a relay to let us know where you were and what was going on," Taylor explained. "If we explain to the other animals what we are trying to do, to rescue the few remaining red wolves and take them away to Ituria's Island before the poachers kill them, they will be willing to help. Many of the local animals know who Ituria is and were very helpful when Knocker was here."

"Okay, my Taylor, then let us proceed. I will let you call to the animals until we get closer to the poacher's camp and see how many you can find to join our group. Let's be on our way. There is not a moment to lose!"

Megan reached out and put her hand on the left handle of Taylor's bike and started walking, helping to guide him in the darkness. The moonlight filtered through the trees, shining some light onto the forest shapes and outlines.

"Brandon, Peter, and Indy, follow us, and call anyone else you find to join us! I will let you know when we are close enough that silence is required!"

Chapter Fourteen

Approaching The Camp

As they walked through the woods, Taylor and the wolves periodically called out to anyone who was in the area, asking for help.

"To all my friends, we need your help!" Taylor called out softly several times. "We need to rescue another wolf who has been trapped by the poachers who have been in the forest this week. Any help you can provide is greatly appreciated."

Looking behind, Taylor noted that he there were several creatures who started following him. Calling out as they joined the group, they let Taylor know he had help.

"Hi Taylor, my friend," called a raccoon. "Lois and I are here. Let me know what you need."

"Hello, Taylor. Monty and I are here!" called a skunk from the darkness.

"Thank you, my friends!" Taylor called back quietly as each group joined behind them. Several snakes, deer and hawks also joined the party. He had talked to many of the creatures in the forest since his adventure with Knocker and made many friends. He was grateful they were answering his call. He needed all the help he could get!

Slowing and raising her hand, Megan signaled to all to be quiet. "We are close now," she whispered. "No more voices!"

Approaching from the east, the cages and supply tent were in front of them. Most of the cages had been put out into the woods by the poachers. Taylor searched through the three cages that remained trying to find which one had the wolf.

Once he saw the wolf, he touched Megan's hand and pointed to it. The cage was on the north side of camp—right next to the one where they had freed Randall. There were several bushes close to it, but so were the poachers!

"What happened to that other one we caught, Bill?" Mitch shouted angrily. "Look, the cage is torn apart. Who could have done that?"

"Mitch, I really don't know," Bill said nervously. He knew to be scared of Mitch when he was angry.

"We have this one, and it looks alive," Roy added, hoping to appease Mitch. "Aren't they worth more alive?"

"We would have had *five* live wolves if it weren't for that crazy boy!" Mitch shouted. "And that silly girl who got them out of the pit, she's part of this too. I know it!"

Looking around, trying to find a way to calm Mitch down, Bill asked, "Mitch, how about if I cook us some dinner? We have all the traps set. I bet in an hour or so we will have those four back again, okay?"

"I hope so," Mitch grumbled. "Make something that tastes good, okay? Do we have any chili and crackers? That sounds good to me right now."

Jumping into action, Bill and Roy both headed directly to the supply tent to gather the canned chili, pan, crackers, and coffee pot. Mitch was always happier after a good meal! The light shining in the camp was from two large lanterns hanging on posts on each side of the supply tent. Mitch was sitting near the cage. The light that reached him was not as bright but still illuminated a portion of the cage they needed to reach.

"Hey, Roy!" Bill called out. "Why don't you get the stove going so we can heat up the chili, okay?"

"Will do!" Roy replied, turning to the camp stove and working on getting it running.

"And you!" Mitch yelled in an ominous tone as he stared at the small wolf in the cage. "I'm not taking my eyes off of you!"

The small wolf in the cage stared back with wide eyes, frightened of what this human had in store for him. Retreating to the farthest corner of the cage where it was dark, he curled into a small ball, not knowing what else to do.

Backing up just a little, Megan whispered, "Taylor, we need to distract Mitch so I can get to the cage. Any thoughts?"

"What if we make some noises to the south of camp?" Taylor answered, also keeping his voice low. "Let's get the raccoons to start throwing things around, and when someone comes over, we can have the skunks shoot them with spray. Guys, can you do that?" Taylor said as he looked behind him, just barely able to see the shadows of his friends.

"We will do whatever you need us to!" said the raccoon. "We can start breaking branches off the trees and throwing them to the ground. Monty, you and Gael can hide behind the trees we are in and spray them when they get close, okay?"

"Will do, Adam!" Monty whispered.

"Very important, guys: don't let them catch you! Stay far enough away so you can escape, okay?" Taylor's whisper conveyed his concern for his friends. He didn't want anyone to get hurt.

Adam and Lois nodded and scampered over to climb some trees just outside the south side of the camp, while Monty and Gael waited in the bushes below, ready to spray any unwary poachers that might come to investigate the noises.

"Nicholas!" Taylor whispered to the rattlesnake. "Please sneak over to the cage with the wolf and let him know that we are going to rescue him; he needs to be ready to run when the opportunity arises."

"Will do, Taylor!" the snake hissed back, and then turned to slither to the cage. Once at the cage, Nicholas quickly and quietly relayed Taylor's message before returning to the group. The loud noises from the kitchen, where Bill and Roy were rushing to prepare a meal, drowned out the hissing sounds near the cage.

"Megan," Taylor murmured. "Once we get Mitch's attention, can you pull the cage back enough to bend a few bars and get him out?"

Megan nodded in understanding. Everything would have to be coordinated perfectly.

Taylor saw the raccoons climbing the trees near camp and waiting for his signal start the distraction. *I hope this works!*

Chapter Fifteen

FREEING ANTON

Taylor could see Megan's shadow near the back of the cage as she stayed hidden behind the bushes; she was ready and in place. He slowly raised his hand and signaled to the raccoons to start the noises.

Small branches were being broken and thrown down to the ground, making cracking and rustling sounds just outside camp. As the raccoons ran through the trees, their movement also caused the larger branches to bend, creating moving shadows from the moonlight, swaying back and forth, adding a sinister character to the noises.

"Hey Bill, did you hear that?" Roy asked quietly, trying to figure out where the noises were coming from. "I thought I heard something over there." Roy pointed to the south entrance to the camp.

Bill responded by banging the cans a little louder as he got the chili cans opened and dumped them into the pan. "I don't hear nothing!" He replied in a grumpy voice, trying to make as much noise as he could. "Don't let these woods spook you, Roy! Besides, it's just after sunset. The night critters haven't even woken up yet!" Bill was trying to keep Roy calm, but his voice was strained. He was getting scared too; he just wouldn't admit it.

The continuous hooting of an owl added to the commotion. "Hooo, Hooo, Hooo!" Shortly after the first owl started, a second owl joined in; things were getting a bit noisy around the camp.

Is it enough to allow Megan to get the wolf? Taylor wondered what else they could do to draw attention to the south side of camp and away from the cage. He needed to get Mitch's attention away from the cage, so he would not see it move.

"I guess the alarms for the night critters are going off, boys!" Mitch called out. "Keep your eyes open!" He took a quick glance to the south but then returned his gaze to the cage with the wolf; he was not going to let this one out of his sight!

Taylor whispered to Nicholas again, "Nicholas, can you go just outside of where the humans are and make a rattling sound? Don't get close enough where they can see you, though. I don't want them to try and trap you!"

"On my way!" Nicholas replied with a soft hissing sound as he took off to the east side of the camp, a few feet away from the supply tent where Roy and Bill were trying to cook dinner.

He stopped and glanced at Taylor to make sure he was far enough away, and when Taylor nodded his head, Nicholas started the rattling, slowly at first, to see what the reaction would be, and then faster and louder when the two men started looking around the tent.

"Mitch!" Roy yelled. "I think we have a rattlesnake in the supply tent! I can't see it, but I can hear it!"

"Come on, boys! Can't you even cook a can of chili without throwing a fit?" Mitch yelled in an irritated voice, then he stood and walked over to the supply tent. "Let me take a look!"

Bill and Roy quickly slipped out of the way and let Mitch enter the space.

Taylor motioned for Nicholas to get away, and the rattlesnake quickly exited the area without a sound. Looking back at the cage, Taylor smiled to himself as he realized Megan had been successful in getting the little wolf out without making a sound. The cage had only moved a few inches, but the bars in the back were bent, allowing her to grab him and escape.

Stepping away from the camp a bit and waiting for Megan to lead the way, he whispered, "Okay, everyone, spread the word—mission accomplished— let's get out of here!"

Several chirps and growls and hoots mingled together in the night, repeating the same message, and then the camp went silent.

"Well, I guess all your little friends are done for the night!" Mitch said with a laugh. "Now why don't you finish up that chili while I check back on the ..." Stopping mid-sentence, Mitch ran to the cage.

"What happened?! This is not happening! I was only gone for a few seconds—where did it go?"

"Bill and Roy, get over here this instant!" Mitch ordered. "Look around the camp and find out where it went! It had to go somewhere! Check for footprints, anything!" Mitch was not going to accept that the last wolf had escaped him!

Bill and Roy grabbed some flashlights and ran over to the cage, pulling it into camp and searching behind it. "Looks like there are some shoe prints here!" Bill called over to Mitch. "Somebody has been watching us!"

"It was either that kid or the girl—or both!" Mitch yelled. "Let's find them now!"

"The footprints by the cage are different from the ones over here!" yelled Roy. "It must be more than one person, like you said!"

From outside the camp, Taylor heard Megan call to him. "Taylor, hold onto Brandon. He will lead you to me!" Her voice was not human, and to the poachers she sounded like a bobcat growling loudly.

Brandon appeared at Taylor's side. "Taylor, rest one hand on me. Let's get out of here!"

Taylor put one hand on the bike and the other on Brandon. "Let's go!" he whispered.

"Man, there are bike tracks here, just like that kid! It must be him!" Mitch screamed. "I told him not to come back into the woods! Now he's going to pay!"

Chapter Sixteen

A RACE TO THE CAVE

"Taylor," Brandon whispered softly as they walked. "Megan says to try and get to the cave you hid in before. The animals will cover your footprints and the bike tire tracks, so they won't be able to follow you."

"Okay, Brandon," Taylor whispered back. "I hope we can make it!" Taylor went as fast he was able, but soon they could hear the men getting closer. Glancing back, Taylor saw the skunks and raccoons running over the tracks Taylor was making, using their feet to erase the footprints he was leaving behind in the sand.

Looking up at him, Gael exclaimed, "Taylor, just keep going. We will stall as much as we can and try to divert them from your path." Then she aimed at the tracks they had just messed up, spraying a large skunk scent onto the ground. "This should keep them from going this way. They will have to go around."

From far behind, Taylor could hear Mitch yelling with frustration, "Where did those footprints go, Bill? They were just here. Which way should we head now?!"

"I don't know!" Bill answered. "It's too dark to see anything!" Shining his flashlight around, he pointed in several different directions. Then he got a whiff of the skunk scent. "Oh, man, Mitch!" Bill yelled. "Something must have killed a skunk. This is awful!"

"Okay, men!" Mitch ordered. "We are going back to the beach. I bet that little girl has something to do with this, and she's probably hiding out there. Let's go to the road and follow it to the beach—*now*!"

As Brandon and Taylor took a shortcut through the woods, Mitch, Bill, and Roy backtracked to find the road, so they could make their way to the beach. It was going to be close, and Taylor wasn't sure who would get to the beach first.

Taylor could hear the animals behind him, sweeping their paws on the ground, erasing the tracks. "Stay away from the road, guys!" he whispered to them. "They were going to follow the road to the beach, okay?"

Once they reached the edge of the beach, the moonlight lit the area a little better, as it was not blocked by the trees; however, that was both good and bad. Good because Taylor could see where he was walking, and bad because Mitch would be able to see him when they arrived at the beach.

"Okay, Brandon," Taylor murmured to him. "I will be able to go a little faster now since I can see the ground here. Let's see if we can make it to the cave before they get here, okay?"

Nodding, Brandon started moving faster, looking over to make sure Taylor was able to keep up with him. Within a few seconds they reached a gait that both could match, and the cave was not that far away. They made a good distance and were almost to the cave when the voices behind alerted them that they had been discovered.

"Look, boys!" Mitch yelled. "There he is, that puny little boy! And it looks like he has one of my wolves with him. Let's get him!"

"Brandon, just keep going! Get away!" Taylor called to him. "You need to be safe!"

"I'm not leaving you!" Brandon replied. "If you stop, I'm going to stay with you!" Turning toward the cave, Brandon called out, "Megan, they are here now! What can we do?"

The growling bobcat sounds could be heard echoing along the beach. Taylor could understand her, even though the poachers could not. "I will take care of those tiny humans; you keep coming toward the cave!"

Realizing that Megan must remain calm, even in this stressful situation, Taylor whispered to Brandon, "tell Megan we will do this together. She is not to attempt to take them on alone!" Taylor knew he could not talk to Megan directly, so he let Brandon's howls and barks talk for him. The men would not understand Brandon, but they would understand what Taylor was saying.

"The wolf and the bobcat must be together on this with the boy!" Mitch shouted. "Let's get them all!" Mitch started running along the beach, trying to catch up.

Flying down from the sky, two owls started scratching at him, trying to bite his arms as he was running toward Taylor. Mitch started swinging wildly about, yelling with frustration, "It seems like everything is attacking me!" Losing his balance, he slipped and fell onto the sand. "That's enough!"

"Hey, boy!" he screamed as he got back to his feet. "Didn't I tell you not to come back here?"

"Yes, you did, but that doesn't mean I had to listen to you!" Taylor wasn't going to let himself be intimidated. "These are my friends, and I will protect them from you and anyone else who tries to hurt them!"

"How are you going to protect them?" Mitch said, mocking Taylor. "You can't even walk without your little bike! You had better get out of the way. I'm taking the wolf!"

"No, you are not!" Taylor screamed. "I may not be the most mobile guy on this beach, but these are my friends, and I will protect them! Be warned that you may want to leave now before this gets serious!"

"Now why should I, here with two grown men, worry about a little boy and his furry friends?" Mitch was laughing at him now.

Suddenly Megan appeared beside Taylor. "Because I am his friend, too," she said calmly. "We will stop you from taking the wolf. My suggestion is you leave now before I get angry. That is your safest course of action."

Chapter Seventeen

MEGAN'S STRENGTH REVEALED

Megan moved to stand in front of Taylor, ready to block any attacks. Behind her appeared Peter and Indy, joined by Brandon, who stood next to Taylor. No one was going to get near him.

"My friend Megan," Taylor said to her softly, "remember to remain calm, okay? You told me to remind you." He knew that she could protect him, but at what cost?

Nodding to him, she replied, "My friend Taylor, I will remain calm and still protect you and all of your forest friends." She waved her arm as she spoke, indicating there were more than just her and the wolves who had answered the call.

Taylor looked around him and saw many of his friends, all surrounding him, willing to protect him. Foxes, deer, raccoons, skunks, and even the snakes, had gathered to guard him. He felt a new strength, realizing that he was strong enough to fight back against these men, and he could protect his friends.

"You are outnumbered!" Taylor shouted to the men. "My advice is to leave now before my friends get upset. They are very calm right now, but we will not allow you to take our wolf friends. Please leave now!"

"A skinny girl, some furry animals, and a snake! Is that what you call outnumbered?" Mitch screamed back. "We can take you and those little wolves any time! Right, boys?"

"Mitch," Bill said in a low voice, "I don't want to get into a fight with all of these animals. I'm ready to leave now like they said. What about you, Roy?"

"I think I agree with you, Bill," Roy replied. "Mitch, we ain't done nothing but hurt those wolves. I guess they may want to get even."

"You cowards!" Mitch yelled. "Look at them! They don't stand a chance! You leave now and you won't get paid. Understand?"

"I know, Mitch," Roy responded. "But it just isn't worth it! Bill, I'm heading back to camp. I'm going to pack up and leave. What about you?"

Bill looked at Roy and then at Mitch. He started to walk toward Roy but stopped as Mitch lashed out at him.

"Bill, don't you dare!" Mitch told him. "You signed on to get rid of these wolves. You'll never get another hunting job if you walk out on me now. I mean it!"

"Mitch, you want me to fight two kids. I'm not in for that!" Bill countered. "I let you get away with trapping and starving these wolves. But I am not going to hurt some little kids!"

"Then I will!" Mitch yelled as he pulled a knife from out of its holder. Waving his knife at Taylor, he continued, "You're the one who caused this whole mess! You let the first wolves go that I had trapped in the pit—*they were mine!*"

As Mitch jumped toward Taylor, Megan reached forward and grabbed Mitch's hand, quickly twisting his wrist until he dropped the knife. Then she grabbed Mitch by the arm and threw him to the ground.

Sitting up, Mitch looked around, dazed, trying to figure out what had happened and how to get the upper hand. He saw his knife was on the ground near Megan's feet, and he scrambled forward to grab it, but Megan stomped on the knife, shattering it into several small pieces.

"What! How did you do that?" Mitch said, not believing what he was seeing. "That was a steel knife!" Mitch sat on the ground, staring at the broken pieces of the knife.

"I told you not to get me angry," Megan said. "I will not allow you to hurt my Taylor or any of my other friends. Do you understand now?"

"Mitch, I'm out of here!" Roy called back as he left the beach.

"I'm out of here too, Mitch!" Bill yelled back. "I'm packing everything up, and we are leaving this place now, and I suggest you go with us!"

Mitch was sitting on the ground. He looked around and saw Taylor, Megan, and all the creatures getting closer to him.

"What is your decision?" Taylor called to him. "It is in your best interest to leave with your friends! Do not make the mistake of underestimating these two puny kids and their furry animal friends!"

"No!" Mitch replied. "I signed a contract to rid this place of all the wolves, and I'm going to do it. I only get paid by how many wolves I catch, and I need to get paid! You owe me four wolves, mister, and I see four wolves right there!"

"Do you really want to take on four wolves by yourself?" Megan asked. "Two of these wolves have been in your traps already, so they will not take kindly to you claiming they are yours!" She was doing her best to remain calm, but Taylor could tell she was not far from her boiling point.

"Megan, why don't you and the wolves leave, and then there will be nothing here that this guy wants? Then he can leave too!" Taylor said, looking at Mitch. "If all the wolves are gone from this area, you can report to your boss that you got rid of all of them. That should make you happy, right?"

"Taylor," Megan looked at him with concern, "if I leave with the wolves, I am afraid this human may hurt you. Can I lock him in one of his cages first, so you can get to your home?"

Looking back and forth between Taylor and Megan, Mitch realized that he was not in control of the situation. He needed to get out and regroup. Scooting back and then standing up, he said, "Look,

I'm leaving now. You're not going to lock me in some cage," he yelled at Megan.

"And yes, Taylor, you can expect me to make you pay for costing me the wolves!" Mitch jumped up and started running away. "I'll be back to collect; you can count on that!"

Chapter Eighteen

FINISH THE MISSION FIRST

Watching Mitch run away in silence, Megan turned to Taylor with a worried look on her face, repeating her concern. "Taylor, if I leave with the wolves now, you may be hurt by that human."

Looking at his watch, Taylor realized it was almost nine o'clock. He needed to be home before his mom got back from work. Under normal circumstances it would take him an hour to walk home from the beach, at night it might take a lot longer, especially if he had to keep away from Mitch.

"If I can get back to my house, I can stay inside, and you can take the wolves with you," Taylor replied. "It will take me more than an hour to get home, and my friends can help me get there."

Taylor turned to the group behind him and smiled, saying to them, "Thank you all for coming to help me. It is appreciated more than you will ever know. I am so glad to have you as my friends!"

"We are glad you are here, Taylor. You have taught us how to stay away from the humans and from the traps they set," said Lois. "You are a true friend." The other animals nodded, agreeing with Lois, and looking at Taylor and Megan for what was going to happen next.

"Taylor, if I take the wolves now, will your animal friends accompany you home?" Megan looked around.

"Yes, of course we will!" shouted Monty.

"We will help too, Taylor!" Adam said. "We will make sure your footprints are wiped out so they cannot follow you."

Several deer and fox also agreed to accompany Taylor home and to keep the humans away from him. One large deer called to Megan. "We will protect our friend, Megan. You must complete your mission. Those wolves will be killed if they stay so you must rescue them first!"

"My Taylor, let me complete my mission, and I will meet you at your house as soon as I return. Guardian will be able to direct me to a location close to your house." Megan looked around, still concerned. "Are you sure you will be okay?" The moonlight showed Taylor standing next to the bike, leaning heavily on the handlebars.

"Of course, I will be okay!" Taylor replied, standing up straighter and trying to sound as brave as possible. He knew that the wolves were in greater danger than he was, and he had to convince Megan to save them first. "Listen, they don't know where I live, and my friends will hide my tracks. These wolves are our first concern. You must get them away before Mitch returns; every minute we stand here puts them in greater danger!"

"Then it is decided!" Megan agreed. "Wolves, gather around me now, and we will leave." Turning to the sky she shouted, "Guardian, we will be ready very soon!"

Brandon, Peter, Indy, and Anton surrounded Megan. "Guardian, we are ready now!"

The blue light flashed, and Megan and the wolves were gone.

Taylor turned to his animal friends. "Let's get out of here now before those hunters decide to come back, okay?"

One of the larger deer walked up to him. "Greetings, Taylor. Please hold onto my back, and we will lead you back to your house."

"Greetings, Francis, nice to see you again," Taylor replied. "Thank you for your kind offer. We must hurry, so let's be off! Monty, if you and the others can make sure we leave no tracks, that would be appreciated. I don't want him to know where I live."

"Yes, we will make sure there are no tracks to follow!" Monty said as he and Gael got behind Taylor.

Reaching the edge of the beach where he would get onto the dirt road, Taylor got behind the tree line and looked back. He was hoping all was clear; however, that was not the case. Mitch and Roy were walking slowly on the beach, heading in their direction, but not too fast. They were arguing among themselves, and it didn't look like they had seen him yet.

"Guys, we have to go now!" Taylor murmured urgently. "If they get too close, you must disappear, understand?" As he left the beach, Taylor listened as the shouting match got louder.

Roy stopped walking and started shouting at Mitch, "Look Mitch, remember that Dan guy who wouldn't take this job, even though he had worked in this area before? Well, I called him a few minutes ago. You know what he said? He said get out and don't look back!"

Stopping to point his finger at Roy, Mitch yelled back, "Look, I don't care what Dan says; he's a fraud. He doesn't even hunt anymore. Why should we do what he says?"

"Well, I'm going to listen to him. You're going to be on your own," Roy continued. "I'm going back with Bill. I'm not risking my life just so you can get paid!" Turning around, Roy headed back toward camp.

"Well, you babies can just leave. I'll get to keep all the money!" Mitch said.

As Roy walked away, he called back to Mitch. "So, who is your next of kin if you disappear out here, huh?"

"None of your business!" Mitch screamed.

Chapter Nineteen

GETTING BACK HOME

With the help of his friends, Taylor was able to move faster in the dark. With one hand on the deer's back and one on the bike for balance, he was making good time. He looked back and saw that the raccoons and skunks were wiping out the tire prints and his footprints, so there would be nothing for Mitch to follow. Taylor knew he had to stay as quiet as possible, so he nodded to his friends and kept walking as fast as he could.

Almost an hour had passed, and they were close to the house. Taylor looked around every few minutes, afraid that he would see Mitch behind him, and his fear made him constantly check, just to be sure he wasn't. This time, however, he saw a flashlight far in the distance, moving back and forth on the ground.

His mind started racing. *Is that Mitch? If so, what should we do? Could we make it to the house before Mitch reaches us?*

"Friends," he whispered urgently, "let's go as fast as we can. There is someone behind us!" One more glance confirmed Mitch was following. They had to hurry!

Although the street he lived on did not have streetlights, his house had a large pole with a light on it in the front yard. His mom had it put in so Taylor could find the house when he was walking. *So I could always find my way home!* He was so grateful for that light now! Seeing the light encouraged him to lean forward and push even harder.

However, as they got closer to the light, he realized that the same light that encouraged him would also put his friends in danger! "Friends, you must disappear now. You can't let any humans see you! Thank you for your help!"

Looking behind them, Francis replied, scared for both himself and Taylor, "Taylor, I see someone still back there. We cannot leave you alone!"

"You must!" Taylor whispered urgently. "If they see you with me, you are in danger! Please leave. I can't let you get hurt! I'm almost home and will go right inside, okay?"

Putting both hands on the bike, he pushed as hard as he could now that there was enough light to see. "See, I can make it home, Francis. Please, I need to make sure you are safe!"

"As you wish, Taylor," Francis replied slowly. "But we will all be watching from the woods. If we feel we are needed, we will return and stand with you, friend!"

The forest creatures ran toward the woods across from Taylor's house, and Taylor continued toward his house. He knew there was someone behind him, but he was not going to let fear take over. He had learned over this past year that he did have strengths, just like Knocker said. Even if his mobility was an issue, his courage and spirit were more than enough to overcome any obstacle!

One last look as he got to the front step, first at his watch, which read 10:30, and then to the street, where one man could be seen walking his way. Leaning his bike up against the front wall of the house, Taylor used his key to open the door and go inside. Closing the door quickly behind him, he clicked the lock, then breathed a big sigh of relief. He was inside the house!

Taylor went around and turned on the lights in several rooms, to make it appear that he was not the only one home. He turned on the TV in the front room, and then turned on the radio in the kitchen.

Feeling a little more secure, Taylor sat down on the couch in the back room. They had done it! They had saved all the wolves! And he had made it home before midnight, so his mom wouldn't have to worry about him.

Suddenly, there was a knock on the door.

Taylor gasped with fear! *What should I do now?* He sat and waited; he wasn't going to answer it.

After a few minutes, the knock on the door returned, this time more insistent.

Realizing that hiding wasn't going to make it go away, Taylor got up and went to the front room of the house.

"Sorry! It's late. You'll need to come back tomorrow," he called out, loud enough to be heard on the front porch.

The handle on the door jiggled, and the knock was heard once more, even louder than before. "Come on, boy. I know you're in there!" yelled Mitch.

"Stop knocking or you'll wake my parents!" Taylor called out, hoping he could talk him into leaving.

"I'm going to call your bluff, little boy!" Mitch said sarcastically. "I checked out all the residents in this area out before I set up camp. You live with your mom, and she works nights. I know you are alone!"

"I am not alone, so you better leave and never come back!" Taylor shouted, trying to figure out what he could do if Mitch wouldn't leave.

"He is not alone!" Megan yelled at Mitch as she stepped out of the darkness and onto the porch.

"Hey, where did you come from?" Mitch said with surprise. "I didn't see you with him earlier."

"Did you not hear Taylor?" Megan replied calmly. "Taylor told you he was not alone. Now you must leave here and not return. That is the only way you will be safe. Is that understood?"

"Hey, little girl, you won't get the jump on me again!" Mitch yelled at her. Backing up a little, he banged loudly on the wall of the house. "I'm not leaving, boy!"

Taylor knew he needed to protect Megan; she would not know how to handle this situation. Unlocking and opening the door, he stepped out and held onto a chair on the front porch. "You heard her, mister; you need to leave now!" he demanded as forcefully as he could.

"I don't think so!" Mitch replied with a laugh and then replied in a menacing tone. "I now have me two little prisoners, which I will trade for my wolves. Understand?"

"Megan," Taylor called to her. "Please get behind me. Don't let this man get near you, okay?"

"Taylor, will you let him treat you like this? I will not stand…"

"Megan, please," Taylor cut her off, trying to remain calm so she would remain calm. "Please get behind me now. I will stand between you and him and he will not harm you."

"Well, little boy, how will you protect her?" Mitch asked, glaring at him as Megan walked behind him as Taylor had asked.

"Wouldn't you like to know?" Taylor responded with a smile, trying to show Mitch he wasn't afraid of him, no matter what Mitch thought. "Well, you'll just have to wait and see, won't you?"

Chapter Twenty

STORIES
FROM THE PAST

"**I**'m not in the mood for your silliness, boy!" Mitch yelled at him.

"I heard you and Roy talking before … talking about Dan," Taylor started, talking softly and looking Mitch in the eyes. "Do you know what happened to Dan? Why he doesn't hunt anymore?"

"Oh, he just got old, sold his business, lost the spirit of the hunt!" Mitch said with a sneer. "I haven't lost my spirit, so whatever happened to him won't happen to me!"

"Are you sure?" Taylor asked, knowing that he had to convince Mitch that he was in danger, otherwise Mitch would not back down.

"Of course, I'm sure. You are talking gibberish!" Mitch scowled, staring back at him, trying to figure out what angle Taylor was trying to get at.

"I was there," Taylor added, as calmly as possible, but the confidence in his voice was building as he realized Mitch had some doubts about what was happening at this point.

"You're going to tell me that you are the one that made Dan stop hunting! Give me a break!" Mitch said with a half-hearted laugh. Mitch took a step closer to Taylor, who was standing as tall as he could, and glared at him. "What do you mean, you were there?"

"I saw what happened to Dan when he had to face the creatures of the forest without his weapons. I saw him beg for mercy from the very animals that he had planned on killing. And I ask you now—what would you do if you had to face the wolves without your traps and guns?" Taylor asked, staring directly at Mitch. He then stood there quietly, patiently waiting for a reply.

"Well, boy, that's never going to happen, so I don't have to worry about that!" Mitch moved even closer to Taylor, towering over him. "Now you tell me where you put those wolves, or you'll be the one begging for mercy. Do you understand?!"

"Taylor, do not let him get so near you!" Megan called out from behind him as she put her hand on his shoulder.

"Megan," Taylor replied, hoping his voice did not reveal his nervousness, he needed to keep Megan calm and away from Mitch. "I will be okay. Please remain calm."

"We have taken the wolves from this area, so you will not find them," he told Mitch. "They will not return, nor will you be able to track them." Taylor was doing his best to look fearless. He knew this was the only way to keep Mitch at bay.

"Tell me what happened to Dan now, if you know!" Mitch screamed.

"I asked you a question, and you have not answered it yet," Taylor replied, not raising his voice. "What would you do if you had to face the animals you hunt without your traps and guns?"

"This is just another bluff, a bunch of lies! I'm not going to put up with any more of this nonsense!" Pulling a knife out of his pocket, he waved it in front of Taylor. "Now, tell me where you took those wolves!"

"No! You will not hurt my Taylor!" Megan shouted, moving in front of him and knocking the knife out of Mitch's hand. "Friends of Taylor, come now!"

Mitch stood back and looked around him; his eyes widened with surprise as he saw several pairs of eyes glowing in the darkness, lit up by the light outside the house. More and more pairs of eyes became visible, and soon the animals getting closer to him could be seen. Large and small, they got closer and closer. The front yard was filled with deer, foxes, skunks, racoons, and numerous other animals, all staring at Mitch.

Trying to bluff his way out, Mitch called to Taylor, "Look, Taylor, your little furry friends don't scare me! Understand? Neither does your little friend! You need someone who will protect you because you sure can't protect yourself!"

"My Taylor doesn't need someone else to protect him. He has me!" Megan yelled. "I will protect him from you, puny man!"

"Megan," Taylor called to her softly, "please remain calm!"

"Why do you call me a 'puny man,' little girl?" Mitch responded to her taunt. "I can take you any day!"

"Look, Mitch, you do not want to get her angry, understand? That was Dan's problem, not knowing when to stop," Taylor looked at Mitch and then at Megan.

Mitch could tell that Taylor was trying to warn him about something, but he was not sure what. Why should he worry about some girl? Looking around, he spotted his knife on the ground next to Megan's foot, and he made a dive for it. Megan was following his eyes, and she quickly moved over to the knife and grabbed it before he could reach it.

"You tried that before, human! You will not threaten my Taylor or any of his friends ever again!" Holding the knife in front of Mitch's face, she broke it in two, and threw the pieces to the ground. "That is what I think of your weapon!"

Mitch's mouth dropped open; he could not find any words to say as he watched the broken pieces of his hunting knife fall to the ground. "Is this what you did to Dan?"

"I was not here with Dan, but Taylor and his friends were," Megan replied.

Mitch turned and looked at Taylor, trying to figure out what this kid could do to make Dan stop hunting.

"Mitch, you haven't answered my question yet!" This time Taylor's voice was full of confidence as he looked out over all the creatures that had come to defend him. "What would you do if you had to face these creatures without your weapons?"

Chapter Twenty-One

FINAL RESOLUTION

"**L**ike I said, kid, that will never happen!" Mitch yelled, trying to take back control of the situation.

"That's what Dan thought too, but in the end, he was begging me and my friends to spare him," Taylor paused, looking at Mitch. "And we did. The only thing we required from Dan was his promise never to hunt again, which he gave willingly if we would spare his life."

"Taylor," Megan asked, "how can you trust this human? He has spent his whole life killing."

"That is what we will need to discuss," Taylor said. Turning to look at the animals that were surrounding Mitch, he continued, "My animal friends, thank you for your support. Your help and friendship are greatly appreciated. I will call you if you are needed again. You may return to your homes now."

Mitch looked with disbelief as the animals nodded to Taylor and turned to walk away. "How ... how can you communicate with these animals?"

"Well," Taylor replied, "as others have told me before, everyone has strengths and weaknesses. My weakness is my mobility; however, my strength is in my friends and our courage to help each other." Taylor looked out to his friends as they were disappearing into the darkness and then to Megan. "My friends are my greatest strength, and I am theirs!"

"Yes, my Taylor, you are my strength!" Megan answered. "You have kept me calm throughout all of this, and we have managed to rescue and transport all of the remaining wolves from the area. Thank you!"

"You never did answer my question," Taylor said to Mitch, "but I think I know the answer. You are like Dan. Without your guns and traps and knives, you are a coward. However, killing innocent animals for money is not a proud profession. There has to be something else you could make a livelihood at where you are not killing innocent animals, right?" Taylor looked at Mitch, hoping to get some type of response. However, Mitch just looked at him. Taylor could tell that Mitch was trying to figure another way out, another way to get those wolves.

"Will you give us the promise that Dan gave us— that you will not hunt again?"

"Well, little buddy," Mitch said, but as he got closer to Taylor, his voice got mean again. "It seems all your friends are gone now, so we are back to square one, right? You give me the wolves and you go free!"

Without warning, Mitch grabbed Taylor by the shoulders and pushed him against the wall. "Now what are you going to do, huh? Your little buddies are gone! If you want to save your little friend here, you will make her give me the wolves back now!"

"No!" Megan screamed. "You will not hurt my Taylor!" Her anger had been kept under control too long. "You let go of him immediately!"

"I don't think so!" Mitch yelled at Megan. "You admitted to taking the wolves, and he is my way to get to you. I want those wolves back. Where are they?"

"Taylor, I am sorry. I can hold back no longer. This human must be punished for his evil deeds!" As she backed away from the house, Mitch heard Megan's true voice for the first time as she turned into her natural form.

As Mitch watched the transformation, he let go of Taylor, who fell to the floor of the porch. Mitch could not believe his eyes! His jaw dropped, and all he could do was stare as this tiny girl turned into a giant dragon, towering over him and growling at him with her long sharp dragon teeth dangerously close to his face. Her ruby-red scales sparkled as she moved under the front light, and her wings stretched out as wide as the house as she showed him what he was up against!

"Megan, please be calm!" Taylor called to her. "He is not worth it!"

Turning to Mitch, Taylor demanded, "For the final time, will you promise, on your life, that you will stop hunting these animals for your personal profit? We are here to protect them and will not tolerate any more of your interference!"

Mitch tried to run away, but Megan easily got to the other side and stopped him. Now she was on one side of him, and Taylor was on the other side. "It really is your life on the line as Megan is one ferocious dragon and an even more ferocious friend!"

Mitch dropped to his knees, looking back and forth between Taylor and Megan. Then he looked at the ground and started shaking his head back and forth. "This isn't really happening. I must be dreaming. This can't be happening!"

Megan roared loudly to Taylor. "Taylor, what must we do?" To Mitch, who could only hear the dragon voice, it was terrifying!

"Okay, okay!" Mitch whimpered. "I agree—just spare my life!" Mitch's voice was cracking, sounding like he was ready to cry. "Keep that dragon away from me!" Then he sat in silence, realizing that he had no other choice.

Taylor looked out into the darkness and called out to his friends. "My friends, please come back if you are still in the area and take notice of this hunter. If you ever see him in these woods again, he has broken his promise, and you need to inform Megan and myself. We will be back to remove him from the forest, forcibly if necessary!"

From the darkness, many pairs of eyes appeared again, all around them. Mitch looked up, finally comprehending that he had been outdone and Taylor had won. Sitting alone in the middle of the yard, Mitch started crying softly to himself.

"Megan," Taylor called to her softly. "Please calm yourself and join me back on the porch. We need to talk."

Chapter Twenty-Two

MISSION COMPLETED

"Give me a moment," Megan replied. "It is so hard to turn back into a tiny human." Megan the dragon crouched on the ground and closed her eyes. After about a minute, she was able to transform back into her human form.

As Megan joined Taylor on the porch, Mitch remained sitting on the ground under the light pole, still shaking his head. They all turned to watch another figure walking into the yard, emerging from the darkness.

As he got to within about ten feet of Mitch, he called out, "Taylor, my friend. Thank you for helping Megan with her mission to rescue the wolves. We have confirmed all nine wolves have made it and are safe! The residents have also advised me of your search, and they found no other red wolves in this area. We have rescued them all!"

Smiling as he recognized the voice, Taylor replied, "My friend, Knocker. I am always glad to assist you and your friends on their missions. It is great to see you again!"

Walking into the light at the front of the house, Knocker appeared as a teenage boy with shoulder-length black hair wearing a t-shirt and jeans. "Megan, you have completed your mission. You should be proud!"

"My Taylor was a big help. I could not have done it without him and his many friends," Megan replied as she walked over to Knocker. Then she turned and pointed to Mitch and her voice changed to one of displeasure. "But we still have a problem: what do we do with him?"

This made Mitch look up frantically. "What do you mean: what will you do with me?"

"Mitch, I have heard you promise that you will no longer hunt animals. Is that a promise you will keep?" Knocker's voice had changed from friendly to challenging, and Mitch took notice.

"I will keep my promise. Just get me out of here!" Mitch said as he looked around. He had had enough of this place, and he just wanted to leave.

"As Ituria's First Guard, I accept your promise and will log it into our archives," Knocker responded with the voice of authority. "Please note we do not take promises lightly." Staring straight at Mitch, he issued a warning. "Do not break your promise, or you will have to answer to me!"

Mitch looked at Knocker for a few seconds and Knocker just stared back, his eyes steady and jaw set, ready to react in an instant if needed. Mitch realized that Knocker would punish him for any lies or deceptions. Lowering his eyes and staring at the ground, Mitch replied, "I understand."

"Taylor, if it meets with your approval, Megan and I will accompany Mitch back to his camp where he can join his other two poachers. They can pack everything and leave the area." Knocker waited for Taylor's agreement.

"Yes, that would be helpful, Knocker. We have identified him to the inhabitants in this area, and he will be reported if he ever returns—*for any reason*," Taylor replied, looking directly at Mitch. "If he does return, I will let you and Megan handle the situation."

"Mitch, if you will stand, we will be on our way. Please do not try to escape or try any human tricks on us if you want to remain safe," Knocker stated calmly.

"Megan, once we return Mitch to his camp and see them all off the property, we will return to Ituria's Island together. Please make your good-byes to Taylor now as we need to depart." Knocker walked over to Mitch, and stood beside him, waiting for Megan.

"My Taylor, again I thank you for your help in rescuing the wolves. We could not have done it without you. Your courage and spirit in the face of adversity were the strength of the mission. Please be sure to call on us if you need any help in the future. We are always ready to assist." Megan gave a graceful bow to Taylor and walked over to stand on the other side of Mitch.

"To my friends, Knocker and Megan, thank you once again for allowing me to help in your noble mission. I will always stand ready to help, whenever there is a need." Taylor then bowed to them both.

Looking at Mitch, he added a word of warning, "Mitch, I recommend that you do not get these 'puny kids' angry, and you should be aware that Knocker is even more ferocious than Megan."

Mitch's eyes widened even further, and his jaw dropped open again, then he started mumbling. "You mean they … are … both … dragons?" He could hardly ask the question.

As Mitch looked with fear into Knocker's bright green eyes, Knocker grinned and agreed, "You know, Mitch, Taylor is probably right about that."

Knocker, Mitch, and Megan turned and started walking down the road to return Mitch to his camp. Taylor used the railing on the porch to get back into the house. Looking at his watch, Taylor saw it was 11:30. His mom would be home soon. He went over to the couch to sit down, and suddenly he realized he was hungry as he hadn't eaten since lunch.

He got up to get a bowl of the macaroni and cheese his mom had left for dinner and sat down at the kitchen table. He didn't need to heat it up; it would taste just as good cold. As he finished the bowl, he heard his mom coming into the house.

"Hi, Taylor, I'm home!" she called out to him.

"Hi, mom! Just having a snack in the kitchen. How was work?" he called back.

"Oh, it was same as normal, but all went well," she replied as she walked into the kitchen. "Any more of the mac and cheese left?"

"Yes, mom. Let me get you some!" Taylor said and got her a bowl. "Do you want it heated up in the microwave?"

"No, cold is fine. How are your little animals? Is everyone okay?" she asked.

"Yes, everyone is fine," Taylor said, smiling, glad that he had been able to save the last of the wild red wolves, sending them to a safe place. While the official report would read zero red wolves remaining in the wild, he knew where they were and that they were safe. His hope was that one day, they would be able to return to their homes.

THE END – *until Taylor's next adventure!*

Note From The Author:

Although this is a fantasy fiction story, the perils facing the red wolf are real. After being declared extinct in the wild in 1980, the only living red wolves were in the captive breeding program in several zoos and wildlife parks. In subsequent years, some of the captive wolves were introduced back into the wild, and at one point had grown to a total of over 120 in North Carolina in 2012.

What started out as a happy ending shortly disappeared. Even though officially it was illegal to kill wild red wolves unless they were endangering people or livestock, people continued to kill them until there were less than 20 remaining. Because of the quick decline in the wolf population, it was recently noted that there have been no new pups born in the wild for the past three years.

Many wildlife organizations and the U.S. Fish and Wildlife Commission are trying to save the red wolf as a species. However, until humans realize that red wolves are a valuable member of the natural ecosystem and stop shooting them on sight, attempts to introduce new red wolves into the wild will do little to increase their chances to regain their rightful place in the circle of life.

Book Club Questions

1. Why do hermit crabs need to find new shells periodically?
2. Do hermit crabs live on land, in the water, or both?
3. Why is Taylor able to talk with the animals in the wildlife refuge?
4. What lessons did Taylor teach the animals?
5. What is Megan's weakness?
6. How did Taylor determine there were no other red wolves in the area?
7. How does Taylor get Megan and the wolves out of the pit?
8. How many different types of wolves live in the United States today?
9. Do wolves live in other countries or on other continents?
10. Why is it important to keep a species from going extinct?
11. Something to think about – if you had to create your own self-sustaining ecosystem, what would you include? Would you want a lot of one type of animal, or a variety of different animals, and why?

About The Author

J.B. moved to Florida in her early teens and has lived there ever since, enjoying the mild weather and abundance of wildlife. She even spent several seasons raising orphan squirrels. She graduated from the University of Central Florida and has spent her working career in the legal profession. Her novels are inspired by her family and nature, as well as her need to escape from the real world once in a while.

www.facebook.com/J.B.Moonstar

Instagram@J.B.Moonstar

Twitter@jb_moonstar

Jbmoonstar.author@gmail.com

Website – jbmoonstar.com

Discover more by JB Moonstar

Chronicles of Ituria

Russ and The Hidden Voice

Taylor and the Red Wolf Rescue

Jenna and the Legend of the White Wolf

Jenna and the Eyes of Fire

Jan and the Secret Cave

Jan and the Search for Lilya

Taylor and the Final Nine

Michelle and the Missing Manatee

Jenna and the Broken Promise

Sara and the Secret Mission

& More Adventures to Come!

The Mermaids of Crystal Cay

Kimmi and the Sea Dragon

Roselia and the Ancient Warriors

& More Adventures to Come!

Coloring Book from

Artist Jenn Kotick

Mermaids

Discover more at
4HorsemenPublications.com

10% off using HORSEMEN10